# Delusional

## TERRI BRENEMAN

## Bella
### BOOKS

## 2009

Bella Books, Inc.
P.O. Box 10543
Tallahassee, FL 32302

Printed in the United States of America on acid-free paper
First Edition

Editor: Cindy Cresap
Cover Designer: Stephanie Solomon-Lopez

ISBN 10: 1-59493-151-8
ISBN 13:978-1-59493-151-2

# Acknowledgments

This book was another labor of love that unfolded with the love and support of many people. I would like to thank my editor Cindy Cresap for her hard work and valuable advice. Any mistakes are decidedly mine and not hers. I would also like to thank my circle of friends who have a wealth of expert information at the tips of their tongues. The list includes Robin Schultz, RN, for her medical knowledge, Ernie Birch for his expertise in weapons, John Dittman for his computer knowledge, Lucy Liggett for her accomplished state and federal law experience and Rebecca Nanna for her unconditional friendship. I am very grateful to all. And of course, without question, I am most grateful for the love and support of my partner, Cat. After fourteen years together, we still love to stay up late into the night talking about the wonder of the universe. I am very fortunate. Finally, I'd like to thank all of the readers who continue to take a chance on The Toni Barston Mystery Series. Thank you!

# About the Author

Terri Breneman was born and raised in a suburb of Kansas City. She received a Bachelor of Arts degree in Psychology and Sociology from Pittsburg State University in Pittsburg, Kansas. While living in Germany, she earned a Master's degree in Counseling. As a psychotherapist she specialized in Borderline Personality Disorders and worked with high-risk adolescents, juvenile sex offenders and their victims. She also worked with a multiple personality disorder client for one year. She decided to change careers and graduated from St. Louis University School of Law. After one year of private practice, she was fortunate enough to find her current position as a Research and Writing Attorney working in federal criminal law. She also supervises students earning their Master's degrees in Social Work.

**Delusional:** The presence of one or more nonbizzare delusions that persist for at least one month. Psychosocial behavior is not markedly impaired. Grandiose delusions may have a religious content such as the person who believes that he or she has received a special message from God.

*Diagnostic and Statistical Manual of Mental Disorders*, 4th Ed., Text Revision. Washington, D.C. American Psychiatric Association, 2000, p.323-325.

# Chapter 1

"I can't believe he stole asparagus. I mean, who steals vegetables?" Toni Barston shook her head. As an assistant prosecuting attorney at the Fairfield Metropolitan Prosecutor's Office, she'd seen her share of burglars.

"Are you sure it was him?" Victoria "Boggs" Boggsworth was standing next to Toni. She was the top investigator in the prosecutor's office and Toni's lover and partner for about a year now.

"Well, I suppose he could have been framed, but he was standing right next to it in the living room and I sure as hell didn't put it there, did you?" She was both amused and frustrated.

Boggs laughed as she picked up their seven-month-old kitten, Little Tuffy. He was a tiny little guy, but very tough, hence his name. His gray fur was medium length, his chest and four paws fluffy white. His tail was only about two inches long, having been amputated before they rescued him. It looked like a little propeller when he was excited or naughty, which was often.

Boggs ruffled his fur and put him back down. He flew across the hardwood floor in the living room, his feet sliding and skidding as he went.

Toni picked up the single spear of asparagus from the floor and chuckled. "Look. He actually chewed it."

"That is so bizarre. What kind of cat eats asparagus? Where was it anyway?" Boggs asked, looking at the gnawed vegetable.

"It was in the colander in the sink. I'd just washed it for dinner." She turned and pointed toward the kitchen, thinking as she did so, that it was a ridiculous gesture. *Like she doesn't know where our kitchen is? Jeez*. A slight movement caught her eye. "Little Tuffy!"

The little thief was pulling on yet another spear of asparagus, and at the sound of Toni's voice, he yanked harder, the spear almost as big as he was. He jumped off the black granite countertop and scurried across the floor, the asparagus still in his mouth. He was dragging it between his legs, struggling with his treasure as he tried to run faster. As Boggs attempted to intercept him, he dropped the stolen goods and bolted up the stairs.

"We've got a *real* cat burglar here." Boggs laughed as she picked up the second piece of asparagus from the kitchen floor. "I guess we're going to have to be careful of what we leave out. Mr. Rupert never does that." She rubbed the giant head of their other cat who was sitting on the island in the kitchen, washing his face. The twenty-plus pound cat looked at her with a bored expression.

"Mr. Rupert is more subtle than that," Toni said proudly. "And when *he* does something, he plans ahead. For example, if he'd have stolen a spear, he'd just lay on it and we'd never see it."

Mr. Rupert seemed a tad bit offended by the comment regarding his girth, but he ignored them and began to bathe himself in a determined and noisy sort of way. Toni kissed his head.

They finished preparing their dinner of grilled chicken, wild rice and steamed asparagus, minus two spears. After eating,

Toni glanced at their large flat screen mounted above the fireplace. "Nah. Let's just sit here and enjoy the fire." She snuggled a little closer to Boggs. "I can't believe what happened to Maggie."

Boggs put her arm around Toni. "I know, babe. I know."

Toni cringed at the image in her mind. The thought of someone being literally stoned to death was almost beyond comprehension. She'd heard of some horrific things in her life, both as an attorney and as a psychotherapist, but this act of violence hit her hard. It was brutal and senseless, indicating to her a mind that had fallen off the edge of sanity. She took a deep breath, letting it out slowly in an attempt to let go of that negative energy. Boggs squeezed her shoulder and kissed the top of her head. She felt a little better just being this close to Boggs.

Mr. Rupert ambled into the room a moment later and hopped up on the couch, plopping down on her lap. He never seemed to notice that his twenty-plus pounds made him a little too big to be a lap cat. Little Tuffy bounded into the room after his brother and joined them on the couch. After Mr. Rupert glared at him, Little Tuffy apparently took the hint that Toni's lap was not available and instead draped himself over Boggs's free arm.

"We're safe here," Boggs whispered after the boys had settled in. She pulled Toni even closer and the four of them waited in silence for Vicky to come back downstairs.

# Chapter 2

The man pulled up in front of his home and turned off the ignition. Even though he was working for God and felt honored to do His work, he desperately wished that he could share the excitement of his mission with others. To rejoice and praise the Lord in public would be wonderful. But it was not yet time. He was getting close, though. He was way past those first clumsy attempts. He frowned at that memory and bowed his head, feeling both sadness and embarrassment. He'd only killed two of the first three people on his list and that was shameful. A task unfinished. He'd gone back weeks later to kill that first prostitute after he'd realized what he needed to do, so at least that was done. The second killing had happened so quickly that he didn't have time for a proper sermon. So even though the man was dead, it was a failure in his mind. But it was the third one that upset him the most. He'd been interrupted and he knew that she was still out there somewhere. It wasn't the fact that she could identify him that caused him to lose sleep, because he knew that soon everyone would know him. It was the simple fact that he'd failed in his mission. She was on his list. He was determined to find her again and finish the job. He wasn't sure if God was disappointed in him for those first three people, but he prayed that He would forgive him for his imperfection. They'd been practice runs in order to perfect his technique. And God had given him another tool to complete his mission better, so he felt a little better about that.

But he had to admit to himself that the killing last night had been exemplary and he was confident that he'd finally hit his stride. His sermon had been flawless and the stone he'd picked out was exactly the right size and shape. He was proud, but not too proud, for that would be a sin. *Pride goeth before destruction.* God had been trying to warn the United States for years, but now that God had spoken directly to him and instructed him on what to do, the good people of America would realize their mistakes and the country would be cleansed. He pushed aside the feeling of failure from his earlier mistakes, begged God for forgiveness and vowed to complete his mission. Nothing would stop him.

He pulled a gym bag from the front seat and cradled it to his chest. Inside were the tools of his trade. He'd left it in his car after last night's mission, but he needed to replenish his supply, so he was bringing it inside. He grabbed his real gym bag from the backseat. The thought of yesterday's sermon made him smile and his step was quick and light as he climbed the steps to his front door. He paused briefly before unlocking the front door, remembering, as he always did, that he missed his wife. He twisted the ring on his finger. She had died almost a year ago of cancer. It had taken her quickly, and for that, he was grateful. Of course, her getting cancer in the first place was entirely her fault. He shook his head in disgust. His wife had been loving and compassionate to all, and that had been her downfall. She'd taken in a friend of their neighbor's after her parents had thrown her out for being gay. At first he thought his wife was going to try to redeem the girl by showing her the error of her ways, but that hadn't been the case. She'd had some misplaced idea of unconditional love and they'd argued bitterly that night. The next day the girl was gone.

In less than a week the girl was killed in a drive-by shooting, and rightfully so. God punished deviants.

When his wife was diagnosed with pancreatic cancer within a month of their argument, he knew now that it was the consequence of her behavior. She died only six weeks later. As he'd sat next to her hospital bed holding her lifeless hand, he'd questioned everything in his life. Tears had streamed down his face and he'd screamed silently in his head. It was the middle of the night and the room was dark and sterile. So many things had gone wrong in his life and as his anger grew that night, he cursed God. He must have dozed off at some point because the next thing he remembered was a voice talking directly to him in that dark hospital room. It took him only a few moments to realize it was God. At that moment everything became crystal clear and he knew his true calling. He now had a mission and a reason to live. He smiled now, remembering that wonderful feeling of God speaking to him in his wife's hospital room, and he opened his front door.

"Why are you late?" his elderly mother asked as he came in the front door. She was sitting in her faded green recliner in the living room, watching television. He was her only child and she seemed stressed and somewhat confused when she didn't know where he'd been. She'd had him very late in life and was now dependent upon him.

He held up one of his gym bags. "I went to the gym, Mother."

"That's right, it's Thursday. You always go on Tuesdays and Thursdays." She smiled at him. "There's leftover stew on the stove. You must be hungry."

"Thank you." He kissed her on the cheek. "I'll just put my things away and I'll be back down." He went upstairs and carefully stowed both gym bags in the back of the closet in his study. There was barely enough room to make a path through this room. He had removed all of the furniture in the guest bedroom and was storing it in here while he renovated. He wanted to make that room into a sanctuary, but he was having trouble deciding on the type of furniture he should buy. It had to be just perfect. Twice he'd purchased chairs, only to return them later. The room needed to demonstrate his reverence and love for the Lord, but it couldn't be too showy or extravagant. It was a difficult balance and he was determined to get it right. He thought he'd finally found the perfect paint color earlier in the week and after a quick dinner, he'd tackle that job.

He changed into a pair of old pants for painting and a T-shirt. After saying a prayer of gratitude, he slipped on a pair of old tennis shoes and headed back downstairs to sample some of his mother's wonderful stew. He needed his strength.

# Chapter 3

Toni arrived at work a little before eight in the morning. She had a full day ahead and wanted to make sure she was settled in before heading to her first court appearance of the day. She pulled out a small mirror from her desk drawer and stared at the reflection of her royal blue eyes. She tilted the mirror and checked her hair. It was cut short but the natural waves helped give it body. When she wanted to be a little crazy, or a little sexy, she'd just put some gel on it and spike it a bit. Today it was brushed back, giving it a soft but professional look. Satisfied that she looked presentable, she put the mirror away and grabbed a file. On Friday mornings she handled part of the routine docket, including arraignments and detention hearings. Nothing that required a lot of preparation time, she just wanted to make sure that she'd reviewed everything. She hated being caught unaware. As she closed the last file in her pile for the morning, the phone buzzed.

"Good morning, Ms. Barston. There's a Dr. Henson on line

three for you."

"Thank you." Chloe was the receptionist and no matter how many times Toni asked, she insisted on calling everyone either Mr. or Ms. or by his or her title. Toni punched line three.

"Good morning, Claire. How are you?"

"I'm doing great, thanks. I just wondered if there's anything I can bring tomorrow night. I know you said that you and Boggs were handling everything for Vicky's birthday, but I feel bad. Can't I do something?"

"I think we've got everything covered," Toni said. "Let me think…"

"What about wine? Could I bring some wine at least?"

"That would be wonderful," Toni said. "In fact, now that you mention it, I think we're a little low. Bring whatever kind you and Vicky like, okay?"

"Perfect." Claire sounded relieved to be able to contribute. "And would it be okay if I dropped off her gifts in the morning? I know it's an imposition, but I don't want her to have a clue."

"It's no imposition at all," Toni said. "We're going to the grocery store tonight, so we'll be home all day tomorrow."

"Great. Everyone is bringing gag gifts, right? I don't want to be the only one."

"For Vicky? Absolutely everyone will. We've got ours. It's the best part of birthdays. No worries." Toni grinned.

"Okay, I've got your address here. I'll see you in the morning, probably around ten." Claire rang off.

Toni gathered her files and headed to court. Several of the defendants were already in the courtroom dressed in bright orange jumpsuits. The deputies flanked the bench where they sat, handcuffed and shackled together. Even though Toni knew this was a necessary precaution for the safety of those in the courtroom, she always wondered if these men felt as humiliated and defeated as they looked. She pushed that thought aside and did her job. It was nearly lunchtime when she returned to her office after first stopping at the ladies' room and the soda machine. She piled the files on the corner of her desk, plopped down in her chair and kicked off her shoes. *At least I'm not wearing heels.* When Toni had begun her second career as an attorney, she wore a suit and heels every day. Now, over a year later, she rarely donned a skirt, preferring instead to wear slacks, blouse and blazer. She closed her eyes and leaned back in her chair with her arms stretched over her head, trying to dispel the stress of the morning.

"Now that's a view I could get used to," Boggs said from the doorway.

Toni nearly tumbled backward in her chair. "Shit, Boggs. Why do you always scare the crap out of me like that?" Although the words sounded harsh, she was smiling.

"Sorry." Boggs was grinning sheepishly. "Hey, it's not my fault I walk quietly. Anyway, why were your eyes closed? Were you fantasizing about a wild weekend or something?" Boggs sat in the only available chair in Toni's small office. "Tell me every last detail. What were you wearing?"

"Well," Toni began, "I was wearing my gray sweats, the ones with the bleach spots on the legs, and my navy blue sweatshirt with a torn sleeve. And get this…" Toni gave her most seductive smile. "I had on my fuzzy white slippers and I was snuggled with Mr. Rupert on the couch watching football. Isn't that sexy?"

Boggs shook her head. "Okay, you had me for a second there. But now that I think about it, that is kind of sexy."

"Only you would think that. So, what's up?"

"I have to be out this afternoon to interview a few folks and I'll be right near Sam's Club. Do we need anything from there? No sense in going out in that direction twice."

"I've got our lists in my briefcase." Toni rummaged through her bag and after finding the lists, she handed one to Boggs. "Oh, why don't you pick up one of their roasted chickens for dinner tonight? I'll stop at the grocery store on the way home and get that chore out of the way. We can have salad and chicken for dinner."

Boggs glanced at the list. "Sounds perfect. Any ideas for dessert?"

Toni smiled and winked at her. "A few things come to

mind."

Boggs stood, grinning broadly, then kissed Toni lightly on the lips. "I must be the luckiest person on earth." She slid the list into the pocket of her blazer and stopped in the doorway. "I'll see you at home around six. I love you."

"I love you, too. Be careful." After watching Boggs walk down the hall, she opened her soda and pulled out her sandwich from her briefcase. She added a few more items to the grocery list then got back to work, reading police reports as she ate.

He was across town eating his lunch at a small diner. He didn't like to eat where he worked, usually preferring solitude, but he decided to treat himself today. He thought about his job, shook his head and twisted the ring on his finger. Most of his coworkers were far too liberal for his taste and he preferred to keep his distance. There were even people there who flaunted themselves as gay. He was surprised that the higher-ups allowed such things, but he was sure they were just afraid of being sued if they fired them. He constantly looked for flaws in those people's work and kept a detailed record of everything. He hoped that it was only a matter of time before management fired every one of those deviants for cause.

He took another bite of his sandwich and concentrated on the page of his opened Bible. It always gave him comfort. He read a passage, then closed his eyes, breathing in the special relationship he had with God. Another message had arrived just the night before in a dream. God appreciated his dedication to the mission and it was time for another example to be set. The message came so quickly that he *knew* the stoning from two nights before had been pleasing to God and he couldn't help but smile.

Only a month after his wife had died, the messages from God had become clear to him and he'd started working diligently on his list of people to cast out. He'd chosen the first seven already and he was working on the rest of the list. It hadn't been an easy task, but he'd been willing to research for long hours to make sure he selected the correct ones. That was important. He knew that God needed and wanted a specific order and he'd complied with that request. Once he'd selected a name and prayed on it, confirmation would come quickly. He'd feel his heart beat faster and his face would flush. There was no mistaking that feeling. He wasn't quite sure why God had chosen this method, but he never questioned his Lord.

# Chapter 4

Toni awoke Saturday morning to the smell of coffee drifting into the bedroom. Mr. Rupert was snuggled up next to her in bed, his head sharing her pillow. She stretched and yawned, causing her huge furry companion to open his eyes and meow. Boggs appeared in the doorway a moment later holding a steaming cup of coffee.

"Good morning, babe." Boggs winked as she spoke.

"Wow. Now this is what I call service." Toni sat up in bed and reached for the caffeine.

"What do I get in return?" Boggs held the cup close to her with an expectant grin on her face.

"My undying love. Now, hand it over."

Smiling, Boggs gave her the mug and sat beside her on the bed. "I've got breakfast started for us. I figured I'd get an early start since we've got so much to do today."

Toni sipped her coffee. It had a generous amount of Kahluá with a splash of half-and-half. "God, this is good. You're hired."

Boggs just grinned. "Throw on some sweats and come down to eat. I figured we'd clean the place and get everything ready for the party before we got ready ourselves. I don't know about you, but I always seem to get filthy when I clean." She kissed Toni's cheek and got up. "Come on, Mr. Rupert. I've got food for you too."

Toni watched Boggs walk away with Mr. Rupert on her heels and sighed. She was still amazed that a woman like that was with her. Boggs had an athletic body, and at forty years old, still made heads turn. It's not that she was a supermodel or anything, she just had that look that made most lesbians turn to watch her walk by. And if they got a chance to actually talk to Boggs, they'd be a goner. She had a deep, gravelly voice that made Toni's knees weak and beautiful green eyes that could smolder with desire. Toni took a deep breath and thanked God for her life. She threw on sweatpants, a torn T-shirt, red checked tennis shoes and a faded red baseball cap before making her way downstairs. She plopped down on one of the barstools at the kitchen island, sipping her coffee. Boggs had prepared bacon and pancakes and she placed a full plate in front of her. As they ate, Toni made a list of things to do. "Oh, I forgot to tell you. Claire called me yesterday. She's stopping by this morning around ten to drop off Vicky's gifts."

"I guess that means I need to wrap ours," Boggs said after a bite of bacon. "Add that to the list, okay?"

Toni and Boggs had finished eating breakfast and had been cleaning the house for about two hours when the doorbell rang. Toni glanced at the monitor in the kitchen from the sophisticated security system and saw Claire standing on the front porch holding a garbage bag. She went to open the front door.

"Hi, Claire." Toni ushered her inside the foyer. "Let me take that for you."

"Wow." Claire stood motionless, still holding the bag in her hand. "This place is amazing."

"Thank you. We adore it. Would you like a tour? Do you have time?"

"Oh, absolutely. As long as I'm not interrupting you two. I

didn't mean to be a pain. I just planned on dropping this off." She handed the bag to Toni, who set it around the corner on the floor.

"Don't be silly, it's no trouble at all. I still can't believe this place is ours. Come on, I'll give you the nickel tour."

Off the foyer was a small bathroom and next to it were stairs that led up to the second floor. The kitchen was off to the left. It was top-of-the-line and featured stainless steel appliances, including a double oven, gas range top, dishwasher, microwave, side-by-side refrigerator, wine cooler and sink. The floor was tiled with gray slate. The walls, painted a deep red, contrasted with the white cabinets. Some of the upper cabinets had glass insets with backlights. There was a huge center island with a matching sparkling black granite countertop. A wrought-iron pot rack hung above the island on one side with three pendant lights hanging on the other side. Five counter-height stools sat on one side of the island.

"This is the most beautiful kitchen I've ever seen," Claire said. "It looks like something out of a magazine."

The kitchen opened up to a large living area. Polished hardwood floors gleamed throughout, a light maple with a dark inlay around the edges. The walls were painted a soft sage green, accented by white crown molding. On one side of the living room an exposed brick wall surrounded a large fireplace. The far end had sliding glass doors that led out to a large deck.

Claire seemed to be taking it all in when she noticed Mr. Rupert snoozing on the couch. "Oh, my, God. That cat is huge!"

Mr. Rupert opened one eye and looked at her.

"Claire, I'd like you to meet Mr. Rupert. He actually owns the place."

Claire grinned, reaching over the back of the couch to pet the giant feline. He returned the favor by licking her hand. "He's amazing," Claire said. "I don't think I've ever seen a cat that large."

"He is rather big boned," Toni said.

She scratched his head. "Nice house you have here, Mr. Rupert."

A gray puff of fur streaked across the living room and leapt up on the back of the couch. He reached out with his paw in an attempt to touch Claire's arm.

"And this is our youngster, Little Tuffy."

"Oh, my. He's got to be the cutest cat I've ever seen." Claire picked him up. "No offense, Mr. Rupert. Hey, what happened to his tail?"

As Toni explained, Mr. Rupert rolled over and stretched all four paws. He meowed loudly several times while continuing to lie on his back. He was hard to ignore.

"I think Mr. Rupert is a bit jealous," Toni said. "He still isn't thrilled about having a little brother in his house."

"Well, we can't have that," Claire said as she put Little Tuffy on the floor. "Can I rub his tummy?"

"If you do, you'll have a friend for life," Toni said. "You've been warned."

Claire sat next to Mr. Rupert and began petting him. He rolled a bit in order to put his head on her lap, then stretched his legs again and spread his toes. You couldn't help but notice his purring. It sounded like a motorboat idling.

"If you think he'll get tired of that and leave, you'd be mistaken. I've known him to lay like that for over an hour. Would you like a cup of coffee while we finish the tour?"

"That sounds wonderful." Claire gave Mr. Rupert one last rub. "I'll see you tonight, boy."

Toni poured them each a cup of coffee from the carafe on the kitchen island before they headed up the stairs. "Please excuse the mess up here," Toni said. "We haven't finished cleaning yet."

"That reminds me. Where is Boggs?"

"Oh, I think she's still in the basement. We'll go there last."

The master suite and a spare bedroom and bath were on the second floor. The third floor had a study, complete with built-in bookcases and a third bedroom and bath. Off the hall were stairs that led to the rooftop deck. Once they had toured the upstairs, Toni led them back through the kitchen and mudroom. They headed down the stairs, past the laundry room and the bathroom.

"Holy, crap!" Claire's jaw literally dropped as she stepped in the game room.

"And it's nice to see you too, Claire." Boggs was standing behind the bar, wiping down the bottles.

Claire inched further into the room. There was a stone fireplace in one corner and next to it a beautiful mahogany bar. As she turned her head, she seemed to notice Boggs for the first time and waved to her. She went to the oak pool table with red felt and touched the polished wood. "This is nice," she whispered, almost to herself. She wandered over to the pinball machine off to the side, then turned to look at Toni's old sectional couch that took up one corner of the room. In addition to the barstools, there were also three other comfy chairs as well as a game table. Even though this was a basement, plenty of light filtered through the high windows.

"This is the most amazing home," Claire said.

Boggs came out from behind the bar. "We really lucked out finding it, that's for sure." She held up her coffee mug. "I was just going up to get a refill, can I get some for you guys?"

Claire hesitated. "I shouldn't keep you two."

"Nonsense," Toni said. "We're almost done and we could us a break." She nodded at Boggs who disappeared upstairs. "Have a seat." She gestured toward the couch.

"This doesn't seem like a basement at *all*." Claire was looking around the room. "It's almost as though there's fresh air coming in, but all the windows are closed."

"That's the air filtration system. It's pretty cool. It's there in the lighting above the bar, and it works so well that someone can smoke at the bar and it doesn't affect the rest of the room. And you can barely hear it."

"And I noticed a monitor behind the bar, just like one I saw in the kitchen and in the study. What's that?"

"It's our security system. We have monitors in almost every

room and there are several cameras around the property. So when you rang the doorbell, we just had to glance at the monitor to see who was there."

"That's really nice," Claire said.

"No kidding. Last week we were down here playing pool and the bell rang. My first instinct was to run upstairs, but we looked at the monitor and saw it was some guy with a clipboard. Needless to say we didn't answer."

Toni and Claire were discussing mattresses, of all things, when Boggs reappeared with a carafe of fresh coffee. She retrieved a container of half-and-half from the bar refrigerator and brought it along with sugar, spoons and napkins to the coffee table. She went back to the bar and grabbed bottles of Kahlúa and Bailey's. Boggs played barista and created their drinks as the three settled back to chat.

"I'm glad you guys were around Thursday night for Vicky." Claire took a sip of her coffee. "Damn, this is good, Boggs. Anyway, I'm grateful. She was still upset when I talked to her after I got home from the hospital, but I can't imagine what she'd have been like if she hadn't been able to come over here and talk about it."

"Our pleasure," Toni said. "We love Vicky and we'd do anything for her. That was a horrible experience for anyone. I don't know how she does it every day. Even though I have to see the crime scene photos for work, which are terrible in their own right, I rarely see the actual crime scene with the body still there. I can't even fathom doing that on a regular basis."

"Did you guys know the girl? Maggie?"

"Toni knew her better than I did," Boggs said. "Mostly we just knew her from the bar."

"I think it'll sink in on a different level the first time we go to The Cat's Meow and she's not behind the bar," Toni said.

"This whole thing is crazy," Claire said, shaking her head. "I see all kinds of horrible injuries in the emergency room, but this just makes me sick. Not physically sick, but emotionally sick. It's on the same level as child abuse to me. I just don't understand."

"I know what you mean." Toni sipped at her coffee. "There's so much negative energy in the world, but for some reason I'm able to somehow rationalize when someone is killed during a fight, or in the heat of the moment. All of it is bad, don't get me wrong, but there's a whole other level when someone *plans* to torture someone."

"You're right," Claire said. "That's an entirely different animal." She took another drink of her coffee. "And I worry about Vicky being out there with all these crazy people, but I guess at least I'm grateful that she's usually just investigating what has already happened instead of being on the front lines like most of the uniform guys are."

"That's true." Boggs finished her mug of coffee. "I'm glad she's not on the streets anymore."

"This guy must be crazy to have done this," Claire said. "But you probably know better than I do, Toni. My exposure to psychiatry lasted about six weeks when I was a resident. But, I don't see how a sane person could do that to another human being."

"Or do that to any living creature," Toni added. "But crazy is a relative term. If you're asking me whether or not this guy was legally insane, well that's a whole different ballgame."

"I've always been confused about that," Claire said. "What's the difference?"

"Well, as you know, the term insane isn't a medical term. It's a legal determination or a word that people use on a day-to-day basis to describe their ex-girlfriend or mother-in-law. Anyway, let's say that a person is found not guilty by reason of insanity. What that means is that the guy's mental illness made him unable to understand what is right and wrong, or unable to control his behavior to conform to the law. And that doesn't apply to very many people."

"So you can be mentally ill, but still be able to tell right from wrong, is that what you're saying?"

"Absolutely. There are as many variations in mental health as there are in the medical field. It runs the gamut from being a little down in the dumps to a full-blown psychotic. A comparison in the health-care field would be from a splinter to a brain aneurysm."

"Well, that makes sense." Claire took a sip of coffee, narrowing her eyes in apparent thought. "So—this guy could be clinically depressed, thereby technically having a mental illness, and kill this woman, but he wouldn't be legally insane?"

"Exactly."

"Or he could think that this woman was actually a fence post and he was pounding her into the ground," Claire added.

Toni burst out laughing. "Disgusting, but that's right. And in that case I'm betting he'd be found not guilty by reason of insanity."

"I guess we just won't know until Vicky catches the guy." Claire put her mug on the table. "Thanks for finally clearing that up for me. I could never get a clear answer from watching *Matlock*." She chuckled. "Well, I suppose I should get going. Thanks so much for the coffee, the tour and the visit, you guys."

Both Toni and Boggs walked her upstairs to the front door. "I really like her, don't you?" Toni asked after closing the front door.

"As long as she's good to Vicky, I think she's great," Boggs said. "How about I make us a couple sandwiches before we get back to cleaning?"

"Sounds great. I'll run up and get the sheets for the laundry while you do that."

After lunch, they spent the afternoon finishing their cleaning, decorating and preparing the food for the birthday party. Toni ran out mid-afternoon to get the cake and by four o'clock they'd finished everything except for getting ready themselves.

He sat in his newly painted sanctuary. The color pleased him immensely, but he'd yet to put anything on the wall. He still couldn't decide which paintings would be appropriate. Aside from the one chair, the only other thing in the room was a small desk where he kept his Bible, laptop and a spiral notebook. He'd spent most of the morning reading his Bible and praying.

After lunch with his mother, he returned to his room and looked at the list of people he'd chosen, beaming at the names he'd already crossed off. The United States was better off now that he'd cast those deviants out. His anger rose as he thought about those people being allowed to marry in Massachusetts and now maybe even California. How could the government allow that? He twisted his ring. It was supposed to be one nation *under God!*

He breathed deeply and slowly in an attempt to let his anger go. Soon he'd be able to tell the world about his mission from God and they would rally behind him. He was special. He was God's personal messenger and nothing could stop him. No *one* could stop him.

He looked at the next name on his list and felt that unmistakable tingle in his hands. He closed his eyes. The voice of God was clear and strong. It was time to give another sermon. Tonight. He felt his chest swell with pride, but quickly shook off that feeling and fell to his knees. He must be humble. He prayed for forgiveness so long that his knees began to ache. It was then that he realized it was okay to be proud. He was doing God's work *and* saving his country. He returned to his chair and began his preparations, making a note on a separate list to buy a throw rug to cushion his long sessions of prayer.

# Chapter 5

The doorbell rang at exactly seven o'clock as Toni and Boggs sat at the island in their kitchen, sipping wine. Toni glanced at the security monitor and grinned. "The party has officially started."

Vicky and Claire were the first to arrive. By seven thirty all of the guests had made their way into the kitchen and living room area and Boggs had taken all the gifts to the basement.

"Okay, kids," Toni said. "We're all here, so let's head downstairs to the bar. Everyone except Vicky has to carry something," she said as she handed a bowl of chips to Claire.

The group lined up as instructed, cheerfully complaining about having to work. Patty Green was first in line and had stuffed her unopened bottle of beer in her jacket pocket so that she could carry more. Patty had been a detective for only a few months and was still getting used to her new responsibilities. She was about five feet five inches tall and was by no means slender. In fact, she considered herself "fluffy." "I can take two things, Toni."

Johnnie Layton was behind her. "Suck-up," she teased. Johnnie was an FBI agent and had a sensual air about her. Her eyes were an icy blue and she had a voice like butter, as Toni's grandmother would have said. She winked at Toni after being handed a tray of hot mini quiches.

Jessie Taylor was next, a rookie on the police force, having worked there for less than a year. Her short hair was dark brown and always messy as though she'd just rolled out of bed. As Toni handed her a giant platter of chips and salsa, she wondered how Jessie always managed to make her disheveled hair look consistently the same.

Jessie's girlfriend Helen, another beat cop, took a homemade pizza from Toni and the two headed to the basement. The remaining guests included Cathy, their resident psychic, and Harriet, who worked at Stray Rescue.

The basement was barely recognizable from its state earlier in the day. The entire room was covered in pink. Several years ago Vicky had dated a woman who constantly wore pink. Boggs had teased her unmercifully, even though Vicky claimed she simply adored pink. Boggs knew that wasn't true and it'd become a running gag. Toni and Boggs had spent the afternoon draping awful pink crepe paper over everything, setting out pink paper plates, hanging pink balloons and a few pink flamingos. Even the birthday cake was iced in a hideous shade of pink. The look on Vicky's face was priceless.

"Very funny, you guys," Vicky said with a grin on her face. "I thought we were just having a normal get-together and not a birthday party. It looks like someone threw up a gallon of Pepto-Bismol."

Toni pulled Vicky over to the game table and pointed to the stack of gifts. "Come on, birthday girl. Time to open your presents."

Vicky sat while the others gathered around. "Gee, I hope I get a Barbie Dream House."

She opened the first gift. It was a pair of pink fuzzy handcuffs. "I hope you don't already have a set," Johnnie said.

"Actually I do, but not this color."

The next box was heavy, and Vicky shook it before opening. It was another gift from Toni and Boggs. Vicky tore open the package and burst out laughing.

"What is it?" Claire leaned over her shoulder.

"It's a one gallon jug of soy sauce. Holy cow, this is huge."

Jessie looked puzzled. "I don't get it."

"Haven't you noticed that Vicky absolutely soaks her Chinese food in soy sauce?" Boggs was laughing. "It's totally disgusting, but it's one of the things we love about her."

The gag gifts just kept coming. Next was a red game show buzzer. It was placed next to Vicky on the table, and anytime someone said something she didn't like, she hit the buzzer and yelled, "Wrong!" Jessie gave her those ridiculous mud flaps with the naked women sitting in a seductive pose.

Patty gave her a plastic toy doctor's kit. "Since you've got Claire and all," she said.

Vicky started to place it on the floor with the other gifts.

"No, you've got to open it," Patty yelled.

Inside were a variety of adult toys, massage oils and chocolate sauce. Vicky was grinning as she handed it to Claire. "Here. Maybe you should hold onto this for now."

The rest of the gag gifts included a giant beer mug that would hold at least a six-pack of liquid. A book entitled *The Joy of Farting*, a horn for her car that played *La Cucaracha* and a packet of rubber checks. Actual rubber checks. After she finished opening the regular gifts, she leaned back in her chair. "Thank you all *so* much. It's such a wonderful feeling to know I've got friends like you. And a special thanks to my hostesses. You guys always open your hearts and your home to us, so we all pitched in together and got you a sort of belated housewarming gift."

"That is so sweet, you guys," Toni said. "But we don't need anything. We're just so happy to have you all as friends."

Vicky rolled her eyes and reached for a large package that was under the table. "Here you go. Boggs, you open it."

Boggs looked at Toni and shrugged before tearing into

30

the paper. She was laughing before Toni could see what was underneath.

"What is it? What is it?" Toni ran over to Boggs. As soon as she saw the package underneath, she burst out laughing. It was a surveillance device called The Big Ear.

"I told everyone that you had binoculars up on the roof, and they all agreed that you needed this to supplement your 'Neighborhood Watch' program. It lets you hear conversations up to three hundred feet away and it can even record for five minutes I think."

"This is hysterical," Toni said. "Thanks everybody. Now I'm never going to get her off the roof!"

"Who wants to help me test it out?" Boggs asked.

Jessie and Helen voiced their excitement and the three disappeared up the stairs. Toni hugged Vicky. "You're the best, sweetie. Can I get you another drink?"

Vicky held up her giant beer glass. "Fill it up."

After Toni got Vicky her beer, she went behind the bar to refill her own wineglass. Johnnie was sitting on the end barstool, smoking a cigarette under the air filtration system. "This is pretty cool," Johnnie said. "Normally I can't smoke inside."

"I know, it's amazing. In fact, I've been known to smoke every once in a while myself and I love this thing," Toni replied.

"You know, smoking is bad for you." Claire appeared by Johnnie's side.

"Good thing it's my only vice." Johnnie didn't seem pleased at the comment.

"And I'm a firm believer in not doing bad things alone." Claire pulled out a cigarette of her own. "Got a light?"

Johnnie smiled as she lit the cigarette. "Holy crap, Claire. You're a doc, for God's sake."

"Well, like you said, it's my only vice." Claire took a long drag and sighed. "This shouldn't be wonderful, but it is."

Vicky joined them at the bar. "So here's where all the action is. When do I get to cut into that lovely pink cake?"

"As soon as Boggs comes down from the roof," Toni said. "In

fact, if she doesn't come down soon I'm going to send a rescue team up for her."

"I love cake," Johnnie said, shaking her head slowly, "but that's the grossest looking thing I've ever seen."

"Thank you very much," Toni replied. "I had to beg the guy to put that much pink icing on the thing. He thought I was nuts."

Vicky kissed Toni on the cheek. "This is the best birthday party I've ever had. Thank you."

Only a few minutes later the group returned from the roof. After describing what they could hear from the new toy, the guests gathered around the cake to sing to Vicky.

He double-checked his gym bag, making sure everything was in order. He carefully looked at each item inside, careful not to touch anything without gloves. He twisted his ring as he looked. There was his Bible, of course. And a grapefruit-sized rock, duct tape, a stun gun, syringe, vial and a bottle of myrrh oil. As he saw the bottle of myrrh, he recited a verse from the Book of Esther he'd memorized months ago. "For so were the days of their purification accomplished, to wit, six months with oil of myrrh, and six months with sweet odors, and with other things for the purifying of the women."

He'd been given this passage in a message from God and had been told that it applied to all sinners, not just woman. He re-zipped his bag and tucked a pair of latex gloves in his pocket. He was ready. More than ready. He'd done his research well. Not only did he know the next person to be cast out, he knew how to get inside the sinner's apartment. Although it wasn't foolproof, he was confident that God would help him complete his mission. He prayed once more. He was special. He was invincible. Once he was satisfied that he'd done all he could to prepare, he grabbed his bag, pulled on a baseball cap and left.

Later that night he sat alone in his sanctuary reliving his latest mission. It had been even easier than he'd hoped. The deviant was far too trusting and let him inside the apartment almost immediately. He'd been carrying a clipboard and he told

32

the man he was going door-to-door to raise awareness of gay issues for the upcoming election. Even though he knew telling that little white lie was a sin, the greater good outweighed his transgression. As soon as he crossed the threshold, with the man's back toward him, he'd pulled the stun gun from his bag and thrust it forward, grinning as he pulled the trigger. He'd watched as the man collapsed to the floor, his muscles contracting violently as though he were having a seizure. A three-second shock always left his victims totally disoriented with a loss of balance and muscle control. With the speed and confidence he'd gained from the last mission, he'd pulled on gloves, dragged the man's body to a kitchen chair, put him in it and quickly duct taped him to the chair. Once that was completed, he could take his time.

He'd bowed his head in silent prayer first. After only a moment, he'd begun his sermon, ignoring the sheer terror he'd seen in his victim's eyes. Once his well-practiced speech was complete, he'd taken out the syringe and vial. The deviant struggled to free himself, but he had ignored him once again and administered the lethal dose. After he'd recited his final prayer, he'd dabbed a bit of myrrh oil on the forehead of his victim. He'd retrieved the rock from his bag and lifted it up high, as though he'd been offering it to the heavens, then in one violent, yet fluid movement, he'd crushed the man's skull.

As he relived those wonderful moments, he dropped his head in prayer, thanking God for the opportunity to serve Him. He felt as though he was getting closer and closer to the time when he could share his mission with the whole nation. He was special, handpicked by God, and that felt good. After finishing his prayer, he raised his head and grinned. *What else can I do to please God?* He twisted his ring. The choices were endless.

# Chapter 6

By Sunday afternoon all of the pink things had been removed from the game room and the trash had been taken out. Toni was downstairs ironing and watching football. She was one of those people who insisted on ironing almost everything except sheets. She was putting the finishing touches on a T-shirt when the phone rang. She glanced at the caller ID and hit speakerphone. "Hiya, Vicky. What's up? Feeling older but wiser?"

"Incredibly funny," Vicky said. "I was wondering if you guys could stand a little company? I'll spring for the pizza."

"Sure. Is everything okay?"

"That maniac killed again last night and I wanted to pick your brain. So far we've got squat for evidence." Vicky sounded defeated.

"I'll give it a shot," Toni said, wondering if she'd have any idea of how to help. "What time are you coming over?"

"How about in about an hour? And if it's okay with you, I'd like to ask Patty and Johnnie. Maybe they've got some ideas."

also told me this afternoon I could borrow Patty to help me on this."

"Really?" Patty was beaming and she pulled her own notepad out of her bag. "My first homicide. Okay, so there were no signs of forced entry in either case?"

"Nope. No fingerprints, no blood other than the victim's and no witnesses," Vicky replied. "Nothing." She looked at Toni. "What? Did you think of something?"

"Not really." Toni took another sip of her wine. She was tapping her finger on her lips. "But, it makes me wonder. If this is a serial killer, it's unusual to start with a perfect murder. They generally work up to that. Do you know what I mean?"

"Like a regular perp?" Patty asked. "Start with peeping in windows before finally ending up assaulting some woman?"

"Something like that, yes. Unless it's a crime of passion." Toni sat up and put her glass on the coffee table. She was trying to remember what she'd learned both as a psychotherapist and while studying forensic psychology in graduate school. "Normally they'd have practice runs, if you will. And each time they'd go a little further until they actually killed someone. The guy would then keep reliving the murder in his mind, over and over. Hmm." She was slowly shaking her head.

"So we should look for assaults maybe using rocks?" Vicky asked.

"Yes, but this guy seems different." Toni was troubled, not only from the hideous crime, but from the motivation. Something didn't seem right. Something didn't fit. "Most of these guys get some kind of sexual satisfaction from the killing. And I say 'guys' because about ninety-five percent of serial killers are men. Anyway, from what you've told me about the scenes, there doesn't seem to be anything sexual here. And that makes me wonder."

"Vicky did say that she thought the guy might have showered afterward," Patty said. "Could that mean something?"

"I don't know, maybe," Toni admitted. "We just don't have hardly any info on the guy to get a clear picture." She picked up her glass and drank the rest of her wine. "If we were talking about a so-called normal serial killer, there should be a clear pattern of his victims. For example, he might kill women between the ages of twenty and twenty-five who are brunettes. The victims represent something to him, so they are usually fairly consistent so that he can relive the incident over and over. Does that make sense?"

"Like killing the girl who dumped him in high school?" Johnnie asked. "Same look and build as this girl from his past?"

"Exactly," Toni said. "He finds someone who looks similar, then he tortures and kills her in his act of revenge. But this guy has killed first a woman, then a man. And as far as we know, their only connection is the fact that they're both gay. Strange."

"Well," Boggs said as she refilled Toni's glass of wine, "if he's not a normal serial killer, could he be a total nut job? Not that serial killers are sane, but you know what I mean."

"At this point, that angle makes more sense to me," Toni replied. "But I'm no expert. And he seems to be able to plan very carefully, so that's something to keep in mind. He's not an idiot and he doesn't leave anything behind except what he wants to leave."

"So it's probably not like what Claire said yesterday," Boggs suggested. "That a crazy person pounded someone on the head because they thought they were a fence post."

"Hey, when did you talk to Claire?" Vicky asked.

"When she dropped off your birthday presents, Miss Gotta Know Everything." Boggs laughed. "We were talking about the definition of legally insane."

Toni recounted the conversation to the others.

"So this guy could think the victims were fence posts?" Patty seemed confused.

"Doubtful," Toni replied. "These seem to be well thought out. And it's not like he just happens upon people. He's planned his moves, I think. Especially with the Bible there and all. But he could be delusional, thinking he was doing a good thing. In fact, if he's truly delusional, he might think that God is speaking directly to him. That's not really very uncommon."

"And God is telling him to kill people?" Johnnie said in disgust and lit another cigarette. "That is *so* wrong, on every imaginable level."

"So this is like someone hearing voices?" Vicky asked as she went to the bar refrigerator to get another Coke.

"It's a little different," Toni explained. "Usually when you think of someone hearing voices it's 'demons' telling people to hurt themselves or someone else."

"Unless you're my sister," Patty said, chuckling. "She's always talking to dead people."

Toni laughed. "Yes, if you're talking about a psychic or a medium, then there's no mental illness, just a fabulous gift. However, other people who we sometimes think 'hear voices' might have multiple personality disorder, which is now called dissociative identity disorder. That's a completely different thing. But with a person who is delusional, the voice is from a real person. I don't mean someone is actually talking to them, but this person really exists. Or, for example, they believe that their neighbor is madly in love with them. In any case, they know who the person is, or they know it is God speaking to them. It's not just some faceless demon urging them to do something."

"Are you talking about what I've read about delusions of grandeur?" Vicky asked. "People who think they're the king of England or something?"

A tiny gray flash of fur leapt over the coffee table barely missing Toni's wineglass. Mr. Rupert appeared a moment later and sat his huge self in the center of the table. Toni rubbed his head. "Exactly. That's one type of delusion. Of course it's not a delusion if it's true."

Vicky gave her a puzzled look.

"For example, Mr. Rupert thinks he's the king of the house. He's not delusional because it's true. That's just one example. Something that *could* be true, but isn't. Like you said, the king of England. There was a real king, or more than one, and there's detailed information about them. A person who was delusional and thought he *was* the king would incorporate all of that information as though it were his own. A completely separate type of delusion would be a Martian or some type of alien."

"Unless, of course, there actually *are* aliens," Vicky countered.

"Good point," Toni said with a grin.

Little Tuffy jumped up next to Mr. Rupert and was greeted with a huge paw on top of his head. He quickly scampered into Boggs's lap.

"See? Even Little Tuffy knows Mr. Rupert is king, so that's not a delusion." Toni reached over and rubbed his huge head. He licked her hand then slowly walked over to Vicky and plopped down on her lap.

"You are king," Vicky said as she scratched his head. "Well, I don't think we've gotten any closer to who this maniac is, but at least now I feel like I've got a better grip on things. A way to think about it at least. Thanks, you guys."

"I'll check on the crazy people who have that Web site," Johnnie said. "Just to make sure."

"And maybe you could check the FBI's database to see if this M O has been used somewhere else in the country," Toni suggested. "It's possible he did this somewhere else."

"And I'll see if there've been any assaults around here where the perp used a rock or left a Bible," Patty said. "Maybe like you said, the guy started that way."

"I'm not very knowledgeable about crazy people," Boggs said, "but I'm pretty good at searching the Internet and computer chat rooms. I'll surf around and see if anyone is talking about stoning people." She shrugged. "Unless you guys can think of something else for me to do."

"I think that's a great idea," Toni said, kissing her on the cheek. "My computer geek. And I'll do some research on the mental health side. Maybe I can find something that's useful."

"I guess that's about all we can do until we get more info," Vicky said. "How about some pink birthday cake? Is there any leftover?"

"Absolutely," Toni said. "And I'll make us some coffee."

42

They ate and drank coffee for the next hour, chatting about a variety of topics, but there was a dark cloud hanging over them. If this guy is targeting gays, none of us is safe, Toni thought. She tried to put it out of her head, but the image of Maggie wouldn't leave her. She could almost feel the absolute terror that girl went through in the last moments of her life. And it could happen to any of them at any time. Crazy people don't follow the rules.

# Chapter 7

The gang was once again gathered in the basement on Tuesday night, this time munching on sandwiches from Subs R Us. Johnnie was sitting at the bar with her laptop in front of her, clicking away with a cigarette hanging from her lips. Patty was sitting beside her with another laptop.

"So what's the latest?" Toni asked.

Vicky finished chewing. "We've got three leads so far. The first two are from the autopsy on Maggie. The M.E. said she had massive levels of insulin in her body and that was the cause of death, not the blow to the head, although I'm sure that wasn't helpful. Also, there was myrrh oil on her forehead."

"What the hell is that?" Johnnie tapped her cigarette on the ashtray.

"No clue, except that the three wise men had it with them," Vicky said. "I'm looking into that. And we got a partial plate from a guy who works at the convenience store behind our second vic. The last two are six, six, and it's on an older model Ford van, dark in color. No other info. The guy said he saw it drive away from the apartment around ten thirty on Saturday night when he went to take out the trash."

"I got a printout from the DMV," Patty said, "and there's a crapload of possible matches."

"And the witness wasn't positive," Vicky added, "so that makes it even harder. But at least it's a start."

"What about the autopsy for that second victim, John something?" Toni asked. "Are the tox reports back yet?"

"Nope." Vicky said. "I asked them to put a rush on it. And I checked with Maggie's mom and she wasn't a diabetic."

"So, that can kill you?" Toni set her sandwich on the coffee table and picked up her can of diet Mountain Dew. "The insulin?"

"I called Claire and she said yes," Vicky said. "She said it would depend on a few things like the health of the victim, their size and the amount of insulin. It could happen in a couple minutes or take up to thirty, but it would kill them."

"Oh, my, God," Patty said quietly. "So she was alive for a while before he bashed her head in?"

"Claire said a person would go unconscious very quickly after an injection, like within a minute or so," Vicky said. "And the M.E. found a needle mark on her arm, so we're pretty sure that's how it was administered."

"Well, I guess that's one positive thing," Toni said.

"What?" Patty's eyes were big as she looked at Toni in disbelief.

"I mean that it seems like he didn't want her to *really* suffer," Toni said. "He gave her something that knocked her out and then it killed her. The rock bit was the message, but not the cause of death. Do you know what I mean?"

"Oh, okay. That makes sense," Patty said, relaxing a bit. "I see what you're saying. He wants to kill them to make his point and he does it in a certain way, but he's not into torture."

"Exactly."

"Now it makes more sense to me," Vicky said. "I kept looking at the crime scene photos. I knew something was wrong when I was at the scene, but I just couldn't put my finger on it."

"What are you talking about?" Toni reached for her turkey club again.

"There was hardly any blood," Vicky said. "I should have known something other than the head injury killed her. Head wounds bleed like a mother. But if she was already dead, not so much. Especially if she was sitting up because gravity would be working against it."

"So that means that the killer would have had very little blood on them," Boggs said. "There's a good chance that we're not looking for blood soaked clothing, but rather bloodstained clothing of the killer."

"That's true. I'm guessing he might have been able to get out of there without any noticeable blood on him." Vicky grabbed another Coke from behind the bar and looked at Johnnie's laptop. "What are you looking for?"

"I'm checking to see if there's anything in the national database about any perps who used insulin as a way to kill." Johnnie lit another cigarette. "This might help us narrow the field."

"Unless there was another obvious sign of death," Vicky said. "I don't know if they always run tox screens at an autopsy."

Toni nodded. "Especially if it's someone like a prostitute or a homeless person, or for that matter, someone poor. Sadly, they'd probably just mark it as a homicide due to blunt force trauma and call it a day."

The room went silent. This guy knew exactly what he was doing, Toni thought. He was deliberate and precise, and probably very intelligent. And if he really was targeting gays, which seemed likely because of the rocks and the Bibles, then no one was safe. She looked around the room and shuddered at the thought that one of her dear friends could be next, or even Boggs. She scooted closer and linked her arm through Boggs's arm.

"I know what you're thinking," Boggs whispered.

Vicky's phone rang. After several one-word responses, she snapped it shut. "That was the lab. Nothing from the shower drains in either place, but there was the same massive dose of insulin in our second guy. And myrrh oil."

"So where did our guy get the insulin?" Patty asked. "Do you think he's a diabetic?"

"Maybe," Vicky said. "I guess we could use that as a cross reference with the plates and van."

"I don't know," Toni said. "If this guy is a diabetic himself, then how does he have the extra? But I have no idea of how much insulin a person uses per day."

"Me, either." Vicky picked up her phone again. "I'll call Claire." She went over by the pool table to make her call while the others talked.

"Have you found anything?" Toni asked Johnnie.

"Nothing useful, but keep in mind we've only got info from larger cities. If this guy hit in small towns, we're out of luck. A lot of places don't share information with the feds. But most of the homicides I've found so far with insulin were done by family members. You know, wife pissed off at husband and does him in." Johnnie leaned back in her barstool and sighed. "And nothing is coming up for the whole rock to the head thing."

Vicky returned to the couch. "Claire says to tell you all hello. Anyway, she said that the amount of insulin in the bodies would be about the amount a normal diabetic would use in a month. Two weeks for someone who is severe."

"So maybe this person is in the medical field," Toni said. "Or at least has the ability to get the medicine?"

"Like maybe a pharmacist?" Patty had turned in her barstool and had her notepad on her lap.

"That would make sense," Vicky said. "Or maybe a recent burglary of a pharmacy? Patty, see if you can track that down."

"I came up dry on the chat rooms last night," Boggs said, opening a fresh beer. "Ninety percent of my search results were about getting stoned, as in drugs." She chuckled. "And there were a few places that were religious based, but mostly it was just quoting old scriptures. Nothing that seemed relevant."

"And there's nothing about any of this on that asinine church

Web site," Johnnie added. "It talked mostly about protesting funerals and some hideous things about that young boy who was killed by his classmate. I think Toni was right. If this place was involved, you'd think they'd at least be glorifying the whole damn thing."

"Can't you guys shut that thing down?" Patty asked.

"Free speech and all," Toni said. "As disgusting as it is, we all have First Amendment rights."

"Yeah, yeah, yeah," Vicky said. "Lord knows we must protect everyone's rights. So, what kind of person are we looking for?"

"Well," Toni said, "this is a tough one. It doesn't seem like your normal serial killer, but I'd say we're definitely looking for a man over the age of thirty-five. And that's just based on statistics. And based on what you've told me so far, I'd say he was pretty intelligent."

Patty was writing on her legal pad. "And do you think he's kind of a social outcast? Like a really smart nerd kind of guy?"

"Again, hard to say. Many serial killers are very personable, like Ted Bundy for example," Toni explained. "But the whole stoning and Bible thing takes this to a different level. I'd guess if a neighbor were to describe our killer, they'd say he was quiet, nice and very religious. He'd probably offer to help shovel an old lady's driveway. And I'm thinking he's rather zealous about his beliefs, which he may or may not share with others, so that might not help us. For example, he's probably old school, which means he would look down upon couples living together who aren't married, prostitutes, gambling, and of course gays. But he might not be openly adamant about it."

"That could be anyone," Patty said.

"Sounds like my Uncle Herman," Vicky added.

Toni nodded in agreement. "True, he could be just about anyone, and that's what makes this whole thing so scary. You read about people who knew a killer and they say that they never would have believed it. He was such a nice man, or he was the Boy Scout leader or something. But let's say for argument's sake that this guy is delusional and not the normal serial killer," Toni continued. "If he's been that way for a long time, he's probably been under the care of a psychologist or psychiatrist. And that would mean he's been on meds. So maybe now he's gone off his meds."

"What about someone who's never seen a therapist?" Johnnie said.

"Well, this is just a guess," Toni said, "but I'm thinking if this guy has been delusional for years, people know about him. It would be hard not to. Maybe I can call my old therapist friends and see what they know."

"So if this guy's been crazy for years, someone knows about it," Vicky said. "At least maybe his neighbors?"

"I'd think so," Toni said. "Probably some of the beat cops too."

"That makes sense to me," Patty said. "When I was on patrol there were a few guys that I knew who were nuts. They hung around the train tracks on the west side. They were always talking to themselves, or to some invisible person, waving their arms around. All the cops knew them."

"But here's another possibility," Toni said. "Maybe this guy has been fairly normal for his entire life, but then something happened. And when I say normal, I mean he's not psychotic or actively nuts. Not the kind of guy Patty was talking about."

Vicky laughed. "Thanks for the technical psycho jargon. I suppose actively nuts is a real diagnosis."

"Absolutely. And I'm glad to help educate you all on the intricacies of mental illness." Toni snickered and took another drink of her soda. "Anyway, there could have been some type of traumatic event that triggered this condition."

"You mean like a car accident and his wife and kids were killed?" Boggs said.

"Exactly," Toni said. "If we go on the premise that our guy was very religious from the get-go, then something awful happens that caused him to question his faith. If he'd had some mental health issues in the past, that could be enough to trigger a delusional state. In this case, maybe he now thinks that God is speaking directly to him and he's somehow rationalized the death of his family. The delusion now gives him purpose in his life again."

"Wow." Patty was scribbling down notes on her pad. "The human brain is amazing."

"I know!" Toni was animated, as was usual for her when she talked about mental illness or the brain. "It's such a powerful thing when a person is healthy, let alone how it copes with tragedy, just so that a person can survive. Like multiples for example."

"Are those real?" Johnnie asked. "It always seemed so far-fetched to me, but I'm a skeptic."

"I was too," Toni replied. "Until I actually worked with one. Me and a co-therapist."

"You worked with a split personality person?" Patty seemed intrigued.

"Watch out, Patty," Boggs said, laughing. "Toni *hates* when people use that term."

Patty looked apologetic. "Sorry, Toni. Did I say something wrong?"

"No," Toni said, smiling. "It's just a common misperception. Most people use it when they talk about schizophrenics. The word schizophrenic actually means split thoughts or thinking, which means that a schizophrenic has difficulty distinguishing between what's real and what's in their head. It has nothing to do with two personalities."

"Tell us about the multiple," Vicky said. "I've been curious since you mentioned it on Sunday."

"Now they call it dissociative identity disorder," Toni said. "The majority of these folks were severely sexually abused as children and almost all of them are women. And when I say severe, I mean horrific abuse beginning when they're toddlers or even younger. And abuse like being forced into a child sex ring where they are passed around to several different adults." She shuddered. Some of the accounts of abuse given by her clients still made her angry. How people could do these things to children was still hard to fathom, although she understood it in

50

a clinical sense.

"Anyway, in very basic terms," she continued, "what happens to these kids is that the trauma is so intense that the brain literally creates another personality to cope with the event. It's just too much to handle, and in essence, the brain does this to survive. Then more abuse and more abuse…and other personalities appear. Each one takes on certain responsibilities and is very different from the one before. I worked with a person who had forty-six distinct personalities."

"Holy crap," Patty said.

"The birth personality usually isn't aware of the others," Toni continued. "They usually seek therapy because they are missing time."

"I don't think I understand what that means," Patty said.

"Well, they realize that hours or most likely days have passed and they have no recollection," Toni said. "And they haven't been drinking, so it's not an alcoholic blackout. For example, they remember being at work in the morning and the next thing they know, they're at the grocery store and it's two days later. Imagine just sitting here, closing your eyes and opening them a moment later and you're driving somewhere in your car. To you it's only been a second, but in reality a day or more has passed."

"Oh, my, God," Vicky said. "That has to be absolutely frightening."

"I can't even imagine," Toni said. "And they may be wearing clothing that they don't remember buying, their hair styled differently and they could be eating something they don't even like. And when they go home, things are in different places than they remember putting them. They might even talk to a friend who describes their evening out the night before and they have absolutely no memory of anything. They usually come to therapy as a last resort."

"A last resort, how?" Patty asked.

"Well, the lost time has probably increased," Toni said. "Especially as they get older and have a better concept of time. Young children don't have that understanding, so it's not as frightening to them. But as you get older, missing an hour might be understandable, but not days. And when your friends tell you things that you're clueless about, that makes it worse. They come for therapy because basically they think they're crazy."

"What's the psychological explanation behind it? I mean after the trauma is over," Boggs asked. "Why do these other people or personalities come out?"

"There's a lot that the experts don't know and I only know a little myself. But what seems to happen is that another personality takes over when the birth person is stressed. The stress doesn't have to be something big either. Or sometimes it might just be that someone else wants to do something or go somewhere. The other personalities all know about each other and some are much stronger than others. The only one that's clueless is the birth person."

"Have you seen someone switch from one personality to another?" Johnnie asked. "I mean right in front of you?"

"Yes, we did and it was incredible. They even looked a bit different, right before our eyes." Toni took another drink of her soda. "And I always say 'they' when referring to them, because that's what they are. The strangest concept for me was when I asked them how they *came out* to talk. They told me that they all lived in separate rooms along a long hallway and there was a large overhead light at the end of the hall. Whoever stood under the light was *out*. It was amazing."

"That's hard for me to wrap my brain around," Vicky said.

"Me, too," Toni replied. "But the one thing most of them had in common was their desire to protect the birth person. The stronger personalities were the ones that were out the most, but after a while, it seemed like they focused more on themselves than on their original job of protection. I think that over the year that we spent with them, we only spoke to the birth person about ten times. We usually worked with the two main personalities that were both thirteen-year-old boys."

"How old was the birth person?" Patty asked.

"She was twenty years old when we started. No one was older

than that and there were some that were youngsters."

"How did that work when a thirteen-year-old boy was out? Especially since it was in the body of a twenty-year-old woman?" Johnnie asked.

"This person was lucky in a way," Toni said. "She was rather androgynous looking, so that helped. Her name was Daniella and the two boys were called Danny and D. After a while we could tell who was who by the way they talked and acted."

"Do they all have names?" Patty asked.

"Yes. A lot were variations of the birth person's name, but some had completely unrelated names. And they were all distinctly different."

"So how do you help someone like that?" Boggs asked.

"Well, the goal is to integrate them all back into one person, the birth person. That's not an easy task. As Danny told me once, he was afraid to integrate because that would mean that he would no longer exist."

"What did you say?" Vicky was now leaning forward, as were all the others.

"I tried to tell him that the essence of him would always be there, but it was a hard sell. I could understand where he was coming from." Toni sighed. "We worked with them for over a year. By the time I left that job, we had gotten them down to about twelve."

"Did the birth person know?" Vicky asked.

"Yes, by then she did and she was doing better. Just knowing that she wasn't crazy helped a lot because she now knew the reason for her gaps in memory."

"And can a person like this lead a somewhat normal life?" Johnnie lit another cigarette. "Or not exactly normal, but be able to function in society?"

"Sure, it's possible and more than likely. Very few are institutionalized, in fact. Most are just in outpatient therapy. People around them might not know and just think they're moody," Toni said. "The family would probably know, or maybe just refer to one personality as Happy Jane when the person is in a good mood. Not that they'd understand it all, just be able to recognize the different moods of Jane."

"Do you think it's possible that our guy is a multiple and that one of his personalities is the killer?" Vicky retrieved another Coke from the bar refrigerator.

"I think anything is possible," Toni said. "Especially if you're talking about the human mind. And although it's rare in men, I surely wouldn't rule anything out."

"Okay," Vicky said. "Now that we've got some ideas for the different types of people we might be looking for, which appears to be everyone including my Uncle Herman, let's go over what we know so far, fact wise."

Patty flipped her pad back to the beginning. "Okay, what we know so far is the possible last two numbers on the plates of a vehicle seen at the second scene. Um, six, six. Also, it's maybe on a dark color, older model Ford van. No prints at either scene. Um, let's see." She turned to the next page. "We know the guy used massive amounts of insulin and myrrh oil. That's it."

"What about the Bibles?" Boggs said. "Can we trace those? Maybe they're only available at certain places. Same with the myrrh oil."

"That's a possibility," Vicky said. "I'll check on that. The Bibles are at the lab and the guys didn't find any trace evidence on them. We don't have much to go on right now, so at least that's something."

"And I'll keep working on the DMV list," Patty said. "Maybe we can whittle it down to a manageable number. I'll throw out any that are registered to people under twenty-five or over eighty. How does that sound?"

"Sounds good to me," Vicky said. "I've got the humongous list of assaults over the past six months or so to go through. I'm looking for anything that involves a Bible or a rock. That should be interesting."

"And I'm still looking for similar M O s across the nation," Johnnie said. "So far I haven't had any luck, but I'll run it through a couple more databases once I get back to my office. I'm sure I can squeeze that into my day."

"I'll check the Internet and chat rooms for insulin stuff," Boggs said. "Maybe someone's talking. If he's on a mission from God, maybe he wants people to know about it. Hell, there's probably a Web site for delusional people who like to kill with insulin and put myrrh oil on their foreheads. There's everything else you can imagine out there."

Toni laughed. "Sick, but true. I'm not sure what I can do. I guess I can do some research on the psych side of things. I've been out of the field for a while."

"I really appreciate the help, you guys." Vicky drained the rest of her Coke. "As soon as I get any more info I'll pass it along. We've got to catch a break sooner or later."

After everyone left, Toni and Boggs sat in their living room in front of the fire. Mr. Rupert was curled up in Toni's lap and Little Tuffy was draped once again across Boggs's arm.

"Do you think it's possible that this nut job only planned on killing two people?" Boggs asked.

"I guess it's possible, but I don't think it's likely," Toni replied. "I think he'll do it again, and soon. There were only three days between the killings and it's already been three more days. My hope is that he'll be so delusional that he'll feel invincible and make a mistake. Unfortunately, for that to happen, he'll have to kill again. Or at least make an attempt."

As they sat next to each other in front of their beautiful fireplace, Toni felt the warmth and comfort of being next to her girl. But that feeling was short-lived as she realized that no one could be shielded from a killer like this one. It's like a suicide bomber, she thought. They didn't care if they were killed in the process as long as their message was heard. And that type of person didn't worry about the risks. It was nearly impossible to protect yourself from a crazy person. She tried to push those thoughts from her mind. Our home is safe, she told herself. We've got cameras and a security system. It didn't help. She felt frightened as the images of Maggie flooded her mind.

"Is your gun still in the nightstand?" she whispered.

Boggs smiled and kissed her cheek. "Yes, and my other one is in the study. We'll be okay, babe. Where's your gun? Still in your nightstand?"

Toni nodded.

"The alarm is set, babe, and I double-checked all the doors after everyone left. We're okay. Come on, let's go to bed."

Hearing Boggs say that, Toni immediately felt better. "You're right," she said. "We'll be fine." She rubbed Mr. Rupert's head. "And we've got two good guard cats. Let's head upstairs."

It's amazing what you can convince yourself of if you try hard enough.

# Chapter 8

The man glanced at his watch. He had at least two hours to pass before his next sermon. He twisted his ring. Since it was Thursday night, he figured he might as well stick to his routine and go to the gym. It was important to be physically fit because your body was your temple. He'd eaten a late lunch so working out right after work would be perfect. He could run on the treadmill for thirty minutes, lift some weights, shower and then grab a quick bite for dinner. He knew a small run-down diner that would be an ideal place to eat. The food was cheap and no one would bother him while he ate and read his Bible.

A little over an hour later, he sat by himself in a back booth. He ordered a tuna sandwich with a side of cole slaw and a glass of iced tea. The waitress left his check when she delivered his food and never returned. He was grateful because she looked like a prostitute to him. He said an extra prayer before taking his first bite.

After finishing his meal, he bowed his head again and prayed.

This was going to be another extraordinary night. He'd been blessed with another message from God the night before. The messages were more frequent now. It was time. He was thrilled that God was asking him to perform once again. He'd spent a large portion of his evening last night making sure that he was familiar with the next person on the list. He knew his habits, where he worked and where he lived. He was pretty sure he'd open the door to him, but of course it wasn't a foolproof plan. He prayed again, asking God to help him execute his mission. He wondered if the insulin was a good idea. Maybe God wanted these people to suffer and be aware of their sins. *No, that can't be right.* The insulin came to him in a miraculous way, so it must be God's way of saying this was the right method. He smiled faintly and thanked his Lord for this wonderful blessing. He felt strong and invincible because he was on the side of his Lord. He had a mission and nothing was going to get in his way.

He counted out his money for his meal, leaving an exact ten percent tip, put on his baseball cap, slipped his Bible inside his *real* gym bag and headed out the door.

# Chapter 9

"He hit again," Vicky said after Toni answered the phone early Saturday morning. "He's been dead a while. The M.E. thinks maybe Thursday night. Son of a bitch."

"Oh, Vicky, are you doing okay?" Toni had barely started her first cup of coffee. The images of Maggie again flooded her mind and she went from barely awake to fully alert in a flash. She noticed her hand shaking as she brought the steaming mug to her lips.

"Yeah, I'm as okay as I can be. Hang on."

Toni heard Vicky give assignments to what Toni assumed were uniformed cops. After several minutes, she heard a loud sigh.

"Sorry, I'm trying to make sure the entire neighborhood is canvassed. I'm going to be here at the scene for a bit, but I'd like us to meet again. A neighbor thinks he saw a dark van parked in front on Thursday night. He remembered the last three of the plate, so I gave that info to Patty. She thinks she'll have a list of possible hits by tonight. Is that okay with you guys?"

"Absolutely," Toni said. "We were going to make burgers on the grill for dinner, so I'll just get a few more out. How does that sound? Are you asking Johnnie also?"

"You don't need to feed us," Vicky said. "And who grills in November?"

"That's what gas grills are for," Toni laughed. "How about coming over at six?"

"Perfect. I'll let Patty and Johnnie know," Vicky said. "I know Patty is working with me, but I don't know if Johnnie has a date or not." She chuckled. "Oh, who cares? This is more important. See ya tonight." She hung up without saying more.

"Who was that?" Boggs asked as she came into the kitchen. Her hair was sticking straight up and it was obvious she just rolled out of bed. Toni filled her in while pouring her a cup of coffee.

"The last three on the license plate, that will really narrow it down for us." Boggs sipped her coffee. "Unless it has nothing to do with the crime." She grabbed a bottle of Kahlúa and poured a generous amount in her mug. "And the theory that it was just something personal to the first two victims is down the drain," she said as she stirred.

"Yeah," Toni said as she took the bottle from Boggs and added some to her own mug. "I think I'll go online and see if I can find out anything more on profiling for this guy."

"Good idea. After we eat a little something, I'm going to refill the extra propane tank for the grill and hit the liquor store."

"How do scrambled eggs with gouda cheese sound?" Toni asked.

"Oh, I would *love* that," Boggs replied. Mr. Rupert hopped up beside her on the kitchen island. "And it's one of his favorite things, too. Can we have extra, please?"

Toni laughed. "I suppose so. And I'm assuming you want your very own plate, buddy?"

Mr. Rupert meowed in response.

Toni put plates on the counter and got the ingredients out of the refrigerator. The eggs were in the skillet and the cheese grated when she turned back around. Mr. Rupert was actually sitting in front of one of the plates. "You know, hon, most people would freak out if they knew we let the cats on the counter."

Boggs chuckled. "I know. The other day when Aunt Francie stopped by, Mr. Rupert was sitting here on the counter. I acted all shocked and shit, claiming he *never* does that normally and that he must be showing off for company."

"Did she buy it?" Toni asked.

"I don't think she cared one way or the other," Boggs said, "but I cracked myself up when I said it."

Toni finished the eggs and made some toast. She put a small amount on Mr. Rupert's plate after blowing on them to cool his breakfast and he promptly inhaled every bit.

"I'm surprised that Little Tuffy isn't up here," Toni said, looking over to the living room. "Where is he?"

"He's on the loveseat," Boggs said as she put another forkful of eggs in her mouth. "He likes to be served. I'll take him some of mine when I'm done."

"Gee, you don't think we spoil these guys, do you?" Toni asked, shaking her head.

"Not at all. They're our boys, that's all." Boggs finished all but a few bites and scraped those on Mr. Rupert's now empty plate. He had moved to the far end of the island and was washing his face.

Boggs returned with an empty plate from the living room. She put it and the rest of the plates and frying pan in the dishwasher and refilled their coffee cups. "Is there anything else we need while I'm out?"

"I don't think so," Toni said. "We've got everything we need for dinner. The burgers are thawing and we've got fries in the freezer." She rummaged through the refrigerator. "There's plenty of lettuce, mayo and ketchup. I bought buns on the way home last night, so we're good to go. Hmm."

"What? Did you think of something?"

"I'm in the mood for Hefeweizen. Would you pick some up?"

"That does sound good," Boggs said. "I'll get enough for everyone. I know Vicky likes it."

"Then that's all we need unless you want something for dessert," Toni said.

"We've still got some of the birthday cake left," Boggs said.

"Boggs! I told you to throw that out days ago." Toni shook her head. "It's got to be hard as a brickbat by now."

"You think?" Boggs retrieved it from one of the cabinets and unwrapped the foil. She poked the icing with her finger. "You're right." She began picking the icing off in large chunks and tossing it in the trash can.

"Now what are you doing?" Toni asked.

"I'm going to give the dried cake part to the critters outside," Boggs said. "It's cold out there, and I'm sure the birds and squirrels would love it."

"Great idea," Toni said. "There's some stale bread in the pantry, why don't you give them that too?" She went over and kissed Boggs passionately.

"Wow. What was that for?"

"Just letting you know I love you," Toni said as she walked away. "And to remind you there's more where that came from." She left Boggs in the kitchen with a smile on her face.

By five thirty the gang had arrived. Patty had opted for a Coke until she saw Vicky open a Hefeweizen. "Are we off duty now?" she asked.

"Hell, yes," Vicky said after taking a hefty swallow. "Damn, this is good. I wouldn't suggest getting snockered, Patty, but go ahead and try one of these beers."

Toni burst out laughing. "Snockered? Did you actually say snockered?"

"Yes, Miss Queen of Vocabulary, I did."

"What kind of beer is that?" Johnnie asked.

"It's a wheat beer," Boggs said. "German. I used to drink it all the time when I was stationed there. Want to try mine to see if you like it?"

Without answering Boggs, Johnnie instead went over to Patty and grinned. Patty had opened her beer and taken a sip, but she immediately handed it to Johnnie who took one small sip, then a larger one. "Hey, that is good." She handed the bottle back. "I think I'll have one of those myself." She headed into the kitchen.

Toni appeared at Patty's side. "You okay there, sweetie? Looks like you're in shock." Toni knew that she had a huge crush on Johnnie. Patty didn't respond to Toni's question.

"Guess Johnnie liked your germs better than Boggs's," Toni whispered.

Patty could only nod and grin.

Boggs was heading out to the deck to put the burgers on the grill. She stopped at the sliding glass door and turned around. "I suppose I should be the proper hostess and ask you all how you'd like your burgers." She paused for a moment. "But it really doesn't matter what you say, because they'll turn out however they turn out. Sorry." With that she slid open the door and went out.

After finishing their meal, they headed downstairs to the game room. As usual, Johnnie sat on the last stool at the bar. She lit a cigarette. "I love this place," she said as she exhaled smoke.

Boggs went behind the bar. "What can I get for you?"

"Rum and Coke sounds good," Johnnie said. She motioned for Patty to sit next to her. "What are you having? I'll buy this round."

Patty grinned from ear to ear. "I think I'll have another one of those German beers. Thanks, Johnnie. I'll leave the tip."

Boggs got their drinks. "And how about you babes in the back?"

Toni and Vicky were sitting on the large sectional couch. Toni was on one end with her feet stretched out. Vicky was sitting in the corner section, with her feet pulled up underneath her. She shook Toni's foot. "I think the bartender is flirting with us."

"You think so?" Toni giggled. "Bet you ten bucks I can get her in bed before the night's over."

"Hey," Boggs yelled. "What are you guys whispering about?"

"Oh, nothing, hon." Toni winked at Vicky. "I think we'd both like another Hefeweizen."

Boggs brought over their drinks and set them on the coffee table. She sat next to Vicky and put Toni's feet on her lap. "Okay, Vicky, tell us about the last one."

"His name was Joshua Andrews and he was a principal at a high school. And here's the weird thing—he was a widower. And unless he was totally on the down low, as far as we can tell he was straight. He's got two kids, both in their twenties."

"Now that doesn't make sense," Toni said. "But everything else was the same? The stone, the myrrh oil and the Bible?"

"Yeah, exactly the same," Vicky said. "I'm going to do some more poking around, but there was nothing in the house that gave any indication that he was gay. I talked to his daughter on the phone and she's driving in tomorrow morning from Chicago. His son is flying in tonight from L.A. He's supposed to call me when he gets in town."

"Well, that sort of throws a wrench into our theory," Toni said. "Maybe there's something else that this Mr. Andrews did that set our boy off. Maybe he's involved in some organization that the killer finds offensive."

"I'm checking into that," Vicky said. "And maybe I'll get a better idea after I talk to the kids. Not that they'd know if their dad was sneaking out to hook up with men," she added.

"True," Toni said. "What about the license plates?"

Patty turned around in her barstool so she faced the others. She got out her notepad and a large file from her bag. "I ran another check on the plates. The second witness was pretty sure the last three were six, six, six."

"How appropriate," Toni said.

"No kidding," Patty said. "So I weeded out any vehicle that obviously didn't match what both witnesses said. That means really small cars, trucks and such. Then I took out any that were registered outside a hundred mile radius."

"Did you take out those registered to women?" Boggs asked.

"I was going to," Patty said, "but Johnnie called me earlier and suggested I leave those in for now."

Toni looked at Johnnie. "What was your reasoning?"

"Well, I was thinking of a case I had a few years ago," Johnnie replied. "We knew we were looking for a male, so I threw out registrations for women. Later I figured out that his car was registered in his mother's name."

Toni nodded. "Excellent. I never would have thought of that."

"I also kept in all colors," Patty continued. "Sometimes it's hard to tell color at night. Or it could have been repainted."

"Damn, girl," Vicky said. "You're sure earning your stripes as a detective."

Patty blushed and continued. "That brought us down to eight possibles, and only one is registered to a woman."

"That's not too bad," Boggs said. "At least it's a place to start. Read them off to us, just for fun."

After Patty had read the list, Toni shook her head. "Joseph Jackson is the name of the guy who lives behind us. What's the address on him?"

Patty looked back through her list and read off the address.

"That's him," Boggs said.

"The guy who keeps repainting his place?" Vicky asked.

"Yup," Toni said. "Now that's kind of creepy if you ask me."

"And don't you think it's bizarre that Peter is on the list?" Boggs asked.

"Who's that?" Johnnie lit another cigarette.

"Peter Johnson, he's one of our investigators," Boggs said. "Been there about a year I think."

"So what do you think?" Johnnie asked. "Is it a fluke, or do you get a bad vibe from this dude?"

"Well, I'm hoping it's just a fluke," Boggs said. "But it's no secret I don't like the guy. He's odd."

"So are most of the people who work at Metro," Vicky said,

snickering. "Anything more definitive than that?"

"Not really." Boggs took a sip of her beer, her brow furrowed in thought. "He acts like he's too good to do some of the routine scut work, but I suppose his investigations are okay. I've never heard Sam complain."

"Sam who?" Johnnie asked.

"Sam Clark," Boggs said. "He's the chief investigator, my boss. Maybe I'll ask him what his gut feeling is about Peter. He can be trusted completely."

"Okay," Vicky said. "Let's do a background check on all these people so we know who we're dealing with. Then maybe Patty and I can eliminate a chunk of them through alibis or something. We'll do it quietly so the guy won't know we're looking. I looked through a ton of old assaults over the last six months. I only came up with two that might fit the bill. Both were prostitutes who had their heads bashed in with a rock. The only thing on either report says it was a white male between twenty-five and sixty."

"Gee, that's specific," Johnnie said.

"I know." Vicky shook her head. "And it doesn't look like the cops did much to find the guy. There was no follow-up on either one. The first victim's name was Catherine Geneis."

"Have you found her?"

"Unfortunately, she died a month ago of a drug overdose."

Boggs sighed. "Well, that's not very helpful. What about the second one?"

"Her name is listed as Irene Levitch. I haven't been able to locate her."

"Did you talk to the cops who wrote the reports?" Boggs asked.

"Sure did," Vicky said. "Same beat cop on both. He didn't remember much, but one thing stood out. He said both prostitutes referred to the man as the preacher guy. He couldn't remember why, but he remembered that they did. That's what made me think it was our guy. I asked him to ask around his beat to see if any of the other prostitutes know anything."

"Well, that makes sense to me," Toni said. "Starting with

prostitutes. It's obvious that not a whole lot is done when one of them is a victim. How sad."

"I know," Vicky said. "It used to piss me off royally when I was in uniform. Some of the guys treated the pros as trash. I mean, I know they're breaking the law and all, but when they're assaulted by a john, they should be treated like anyone else."

"I agree with you, Vicky. Makes me mad." Toni finished her beer and got up to get another. "Anyone else?" Vicky and Boggs nodded. Toni went behind the bar. "How about you two? Ready for another round? I heard Johnnie was buying." After getting everyone fresh drinks, Toni returned to the couch.

"So it looks like our guy is on at least number five," Toni said after sitting back down. "And he waited five days, so maybe that's not an indicator. I would like to check the dates on all five to see if there's anything significant though."

"Good idea," Vicky said. "For all we know they could be obscure religious holidays."

"Exactly," Toni said. "There's got to be a connection. The first two could have been somewhat random if he was practicing, but these murders are definitely planned. If we could only figure out what he's thinking, maybe we could get one step ahead of him."

"Well, I came up dry with burglaries of pharmacies or medical supply places," Patty said. "I went out two hundred and fifty miles. Nothing."

"So that means he's getting his insulin somewhere else," Johnnie said. "What about at a hospital? Maybe it's someone who works there who's pilfering the stuff in small amounts. You know, like a vial every couple weeks."

"I'm not sure how the access to meds works," Vicky said. "I'm sure that the heavy-duty narcotics are strictly watched, but who knows about insulin. I'll ask Claire. She's worked in two hospitals, so she probably knows the routine." Vicky flipped open her phone and wandered over to the other side of the room and plopped down on one of the overstuffed chairs.

While they waited for her to finish her call, Toni leaned

closer to Boggs and whispered in her ear. "What do you think about those two?"

Boggs looked at Johnnie and Patty sitting at the bar. Johnnie had pulled her laptop from her messenger bag and it was between them on the bar. They were only inches apart.

"It looks like Johnnie is about to make Patty's dream come true," Boggs whispered back. "What the hell are they looking at?"

"No clue." Toni giggled. "Jeez. I've got one hell of a buzz. I don't remember beer doing this to me."

"It's nine percent alcohol," Boggs said. "Not like regular American beer." She nuzzled Toni's neck. "How about us kicking these guys out?"

Toni kissed Boggs. "I love that about us. After being together a year, we still can't keep our hands off each other. But if you can hang on a little bit, I'll let you drive me home after they leave." She giggled again at her own humor and turned her attention to the bar. "Hey, you guys. Whatcha doin'?" There was no response. She watched as Johnnie whispered something in Patty's ear.

"Hey, you guys!" This time she yelled a bit, causing both of them to turn around. She noticed that Patty's face was flushed.

"Johnnie's got the coolest game on her computer," Patty said quickly, in an obvious attempt to cover her embarrassment. "You play a detective named Fred Firebrand and help him solve a murder. They show you the crime scene and the suspects. It's animated, so it's not really gross or anything." She was talking fast.

"I heard that was actually a great training tool," Vicky said as she rejoined the group. "Claire says to tell you all hello. She wished she could be here instead of at the hospital." Vicky sat next to Mr. Rupert on the couch and scratched his head. "She said that insulin isn't watched that carefully in the hospital and lots of folks could have access. Narcotics are under lock and key and have to be carefully logged when used, but insulin not so much. There's some control, of course, but shortages wouldn't come under the same type of scrutiny." She sipped her beer. "So I guess that leaves hospital employees on the list of possibilities."

"Did you ever find out anything about the Bibles or the myrrh oil?" Toni stretched her feet out and put them on the coffee table.

"The only thing we know about these particular Bibles are that they're usually sold in bulk to churches and motels and such. You can't tell which shipment these came in according to the publisher, but at least we know that he didn't go in a bookstore and order them. Maybe he took them from a motel or something." Vicky shrugged.

"But wouldn't they have the name of the motel stamped in them?" Patty asked.

"Hmm. Not sure on that one," Vicky said.

"And the myrrh oil?" Toni asked.

"It has a lot of therapeutic qualities," Vicky said. "It can be used as an anti-inflammatory, antiseptic, expectorant, for mouth ulcers—a bunch of stuff. All three of the health food stores in town carry it. Maybe when we finally get a manageable number of suspects we can show their pictures around. Otherwise, no good leads there."

"Gee, who knew," Johnnie said as she lit a cigarette. "I think I should pick up a bottle myself. What did you do, go to all-about-myrrh dot com?"

"Sure did," Vicky said. "Right after I saw your picture on asswipes dot com."

Toni giggled again.

"Good one." Johnnie raised her glass of rum and Coke. She looked over at Toni. "I think you got your date drunk," Johnnie said, winking at Boggs.

"She told me I could drive her home after you guys left," Boggs said. "I think I might even get lucky."

"You'll be lucky if she doesn't pass out on you," Johnnie said.

"Hello? I'm in the room here. Just because I'm tippy doesn't mean you can talk about me like I'm not here." Toni grinned.

"Tippy?" Vicky laughed.

"Yes, tippy," Toni said. "That's a little more than buzzed, but not drunk."

They all laughed. "Well, Tippy, I guess that's enough thinking for tonight then," Vicky said, glancing at her watch. "I think I'll head home. Claire gets off work in about a half hour and I want to have enough time to shower before she gets to my place."

"Maybe you should wait until she gets there and invite her to join you," Johnnie said.

"Hmm. Not a bad idea." Vicky stood to leave. "Who knew you were such a romantic."

"I have my moments," Johnnie said. She shut down her laptop and put it in her messenger bag. She drained the last of her rum and Coke and smiled at Patty. "Want to finish playing Detective Firebrand at my place?"

Patty's eyes doubled in size and she merely nodded to the offer from Johnnie. Toni and Boggs walked their guests to the front door, setting the alarm after they left.

"What do you think about those two?" Boggs asked as she turned off lights in the living room.

Toni leaned against the kitchen island watching Boggs. "Well, I know that Patty has had a crush on Johnnie for years." She sipped at her bottle of water. "I'm only hoping that if Johnnie makes a move, she's serious. She's such a player. I don't want Patty to get hurt."

"I think Patty knows that. Hopefully if they hook up, Patty will know that it's not a long-term thing. I'd hate to see her get hurt too. Plus, that would make for some pretty awkward get-togethers." She turned off the last light and wrapped her arms around Toni's waist. "Ready for bed, babe?"

Toni tried to suppress a yawn. "Absolutely."

Boggs laughed. "Actually, I'm pretty tired myself. Why don't we just go upstairs and snuggle until we fall to sleep?" She yawned herself. "At this rate, it should take about two minutes." She took Toni's hand in hers and led her up the stairs to their bedroom. Boggs took out a pair of jammies from the drawer and tossed them to her. "Here you go, babe." She stripped off her own clothing and pulled on an oversized T-shirt. By the time Boggs came out of the bathroom Toni was already under the covers.

"I think there's room for you in here," Toni said, patting the bed. Mr. Rupert and Little Tuffy were already tucked in at the top of the bed.

"Even though I had other ideas earlier this evening, I think this is wonderful," Boggs said as she slid under the covers. She pulled Toni to her and wrapped her arms around her, careful not to disturb either of the boys. They fit together perfectly.

"I agree." Toni turned her head to kiss Boggs, then settled back down in her arms. "I could stay like this forever." Before she drifted off to sleep, she realized how lucky she was to have Boggs in her life and for the moment, she felt safe.

# Chapter 10

Toni and Boggs were lounging in their living room at around ten on Sunday morning. Toni had awakened early and they'd made the most of the early morning hours. After showering, Boggs had run out and gotten them breakfast at Hardee's and lattés from Starbucks. Toni had finished her bacon, egg and cheese biscuit and was working on the Sunday crossword puzzle when the doorbell rang.

"Who the hell could that be?" Boggs checked the monitor in the kitchen. "It's the whole gang, for God's sake. I'm not letting them in."

Toni just smiled and shook her head.

Boggs sighed and opened the door. "This better be good."

Vicky barged past her with a cardboard container holding five large cups of coffee from Starbucks. "Since this was a bit unplanned, I figured I'd stop by Starbuckets." She looked at the cups already on the coffee table.

Toni held out her hand. "I finished mine a half hour ago." She put the newspaper on the floor. "I love that you call it Starbuckets. Make yourself comfy, you guys."

"Here," Vicky said, pulling a cup from the holder and looking at the writing on the side. "This is a triple venti low-fat latté." She looked at the other cups before handing one to Boggs. "Same for you." She pulled a third for Patty. "Here, this one has sugar," she said. "And I was clueless for you, Johnnie, so I got plain black. It sounded butch." She was grinning as she handed the cup over.

"Actually that's perfect," Johnnie said. "Thanks."

Toni and Boggs sat on their couch with Vicky and Patty each taking one of the leather club chairs. Toni noticed that Patty was wearing the same clothing she had on last night and couldn't help but smile. Johnnie pulled one of the oversized ottomans over and sat near Patty. She had her messenger bag with her.

"So what's the big emergency?" Boggs asked, sipping her coffee. "Jeez, I should be bouncing off the walls by noon."

"Okay," Vicky began. "I met with Joshua Andrews's two kids this morning. The daughter is obviously distraught, but seemed very organized. I let them inside their dad's house and she began an inventory to check and see if anything was stolen. I think she was still in shock, but she was doing what she thought she could."

"What about the son?" Toni had removed the lid to her coffee and was blowing on the hot liquid.

"Get this," Vicky said, grinning. "The boy is a total flamer, but incredibly sweet. And here's the kicker. He said his dad was very active in Fairfield's PFLAG organization."

"Ah, well, that makes sense," Toni said.

"Sure, that's what I thought. That's why I called Patty." She looked over at a now blushing Patty.

Before anyone could make a comment, Johnnie spoke. "Yes, it's my fault that Patty didn't finish the background checks last night," she said. "We played Detective Firebrand really late and then we got too tired."

Toni thought she looked almost embarrassed. "Been there, done that," Toni replied. "I was so tired last night I barely made it up to our bedroom."

"But we finished them all this morning," Johnnie continued. She took her laptop out of her messenger bag and booted it up.

Patty was grinning and nodding.

"Cool," Toni said, smiling back at Patty and giving her a quick wink. "Well, we can assume that our killer is still on the anti-gay thing, since Mr. Andrews was an active member and parent of a gay son. At least we may have the connection. The next question is figuring out how he picks his victims. There are a lot of gays and lesbians in Fairfield and even more friends and parents of gays. We've got to figure out his pattern."

Patty took Johnnie's laptop and started typing. After a few moments, she spoke. "Okay, we ran backgrounds on the eight possible hits from the license plates. We were able to throw out four of those. Three of those have moved out of state and one was totaled about a month ago."

"Perfect. Let's hear the names of the ones who are left," Vicky said.

"Joe Jackson, the weird neighbor," Patty said.

"Great," Boggs said. "We might have a lunatic living behind us?"

"It gets better," Patty said. "Peter Johnson, your favorite investigator, Charlie Jones and David Davidson."

"Who in the hell names their kid David Davidson?" Toni asked. "Shouldn't there be a law against repetitive names?"

Vicky rolled her eyes.

"And Charlie Jones is an ex-cop," Patty added. "He was on the job until about six years ago."

"I remember him, good cop. He was shot a few times by some punk. He took medical retirement," Vicky said.

"Do you think he went crazy?" Boggs asked.

Vicky thought for a moment. "I didn't know him that well, only by reputation, but I haven't heard anything strange about him."

"His van is registered to him and to Help Services," Patty added. "It's a shelter and mental health clinic."

74

"Then maybe someone at the shelter used the van," Toni said.

"I'll call Charlie tomorrow and set up a meeting with him. Maybe he can think of someone there who might have taken the van."

"What about this David Davidson dude?" Boggs asked. "What's his story?"

"We don't know much yet," Patty said. "He's a salesman for a pharmaceutical company."

"Hmm. That might give him access to the insulin," Toni said.

"That's what I was thinking," Johnnie added, sipping at her coffee. "I'm going to stop by my office after we leave here and do a full background check on all these guys. Maybe something will pop up."

"I'm sure Peter will come up clean," Boggs said. "I mean he's working for us. I think I'll have a chat with Sam and see what turns up."

"What do you know about Joe Jackson?" Toni asked.

"Aside from owning a van," Patty said, "not much. He works at the county library as an archives specialist, whatever that means. None of our suspects has any priors. A bunch of law-abiding citizens."

"At least we've got some suspects in mind," Toni said. "But what really bothers me is how he's picking his victims. There's got to be something that we're missing here. We've got the two prostitutes, because I'm almost positive those are connected, Maggie, the bookstore owner and the dad. The last three had ties to the gay and lesbian community and the prostitutes were, well, prostitutes. This guy seems too precise to just pick random folks. There's got to be something there, and we're just not seeing it."

"Maybe after we've done a thorough background," Vicky said. "It could be something as simple as attending the same high school or having the same dentist."

Toni nodded. She took another sip of her coffee. "Wow. Having the same doctor or dentist, now there's an angle that might make sense. A crazy doc. Well, whatever the hell it is, it has to be *very* significant to our killer. Once we find that, we should be able to figure out who he's targeting next and why."

"Sounds like quite a long shot," Johnnie said. "But I'll dig up as much as I can."

Vicky closed her notepad. "Here's the plan. I'll call Charlie this afternoon and set up a meeting with him. Johnnie will do the FBI thing." She grinned. "Who knows what you feds have at your disposal."

Johnnie smiled and rolled her eyes.

"Boggs, you talk to Sam and dig a bit in Peter's world," Vicky continued. "Patty, you see what you can find out about Mr. Weird Neighbor and the salesman."

"What about me?" Toni asked.

Vicky narrowed her eyes in thought. "Hmm. I know, maybe you could find out about this shelter that Charlie works at. What kind of clients are we looking at and stuff like that."

"Okay, I can do that," Toni said. "Not nearly as fun as your jobs, but I can do that."

"That's what you get for passing up working at the Bureau," Johnnie said, giving Toni a quick wink.

Toni laughed. "Maybe you're right. My favorite part of being an attorney is finding the missing pieces."

The gang chatted for a bit, finishing their huge cups of coffee. By the time they left, Toni was thinking more about the upcoming football games for the day instead of a serial killer out on the loose.

# Chapter 11

Toni arrived at the office a little earlier than normal on Monday morning. She had a motion hearing on one of her burglary cases and wanted to be prepared. She hung up her trench coat on her tiny and wobbly coatrack and glanced at her reflection in the small mirror behind her door. It was barely big enough for her to see her entire head. She checked her hair, earrings and teeth. All accounted for and everything looked fine, but she ran her fingers through her hair anyway. She was wearing her favorite gray wool slacks, matching blazer and a white silk blouse. I actually look like a lawyer today, she thought.

She removed her blazer and looked at the coatrack. There was no way in hell it would handle both her coat and blazer. She sighed and hung her blazer carefully over the only spare chair in her office before sitting at her desk. As usual, it was piled high with various files and statute books. She pulled out the file for the hearing and reread her notes, making a few additions here and there.

The defense counsel had filed a motion to suppress evidence and statements made by the defendant. He argued that the consent to search was involuntary because the defendant only had a sixth-grade education. Although that was a valid argument, the defense failed to point out that the defendant had been arrested almost twenty times and knew the procedure better than most rookie cops. He'd been given his Miranda rights, and as far as she could see, the police officers did everything strictly by the book in this case. She doubted the hearing would last more than fifteen minutes.

She glanced over the case law she'd printed on Friday, making sure she knew the facts of each case by heart. It wasn't as though this was a life-or-death hearing, but she liked to be prepared. She was still new at this job, only working at Metro for a little over a year. After about twenty minutes, she slipped on her blazer, picked up her files and headed to the courtroom.

Boggs was standing at the soda machine when she saw Toni leave her office and head off in the opposite direction. She was grinning and her eyes were glued to Toni's backside.

"It's not like you haven't seen that before," Sam Clark said, grinning. He reached down and retrieved his Diet Coke from the machine. He popped open the can and took several gulps.

Boggs didn't stop looking at Toni until she disappeared around the corner. "Some things never get old," she replied. She watched her boss take several more gulps of soda before putting another dollar in the machine. She grabbed the next can of Diet Coke as it fell into the slot. "I'll hold this one for you so you can continue to drink that one while we walk to your office." She grinned and shook her head. She followed him around the corner to his office, closing the door behind her.

"What's up?" Sam finished off the can and tossed it in the nearly full small blue recycle bin next to his desk. He held out his hand for the other soda. He was nearing sixty years old and his gray hair was cropped short. He was a little rotund and had an ever-present smile on his face. He was one of the few veterans of the office that still had an optimistic outlook on life. He was seldom seen without a Diet Coke clutched in his hand.

Boggs handed him the second soda. "I want to talk to you about Peter," she began. "Not the usual crap, like he drives me nuts, but I want to know what you really think about him."

"Something I should know about?" Sam opened the new can and took another swig before setting it down on his desk.

"Vicky's working a serial murder case," she said, stretching her legs out in front of her. "His van matches the suspect vehicle."

"Anything else?" Sam's face gave away nothing.

"Aside from the fact that I think he avoids scut work and he barely speaks to me? No. That's it."

Sam dug through some files in his desk drawer. He pulled out one folder and handed it to Boggs. "Here. This is my personnel file on him. Nothing official. If it were anyone but you, I'd tell you to go to hell. But I know you, and you wouldn't be asking if there wasn't something there."

Boggs took the file. "Thanks, Sam. I appreciate that."

"Off the record?" Sam took another slug of his soda.

"Sure."

"I don't like the guy. He does his job, but only the bare minimum. And I don't like the way he treats you or some of the attorneys. It's like he's better than everyone else. It's nothing specific, you know. Nothing I could point my finger at and call him on it. But it's just that underlying attitude that rubs me the wrong way. I feel like he's rolling his eyes at me when I ask him to do something. He's not, of course, but it *feels* like he is. If I had a real reason to fire him, I would."

"I know exactly what you mean," Boggs said. She glanced at the file on her lap. "I'm going to snoop a little, but nothing out in the open. I'll let you know what I find out." She stood to leave. "And by the way, you owe me lunch today. The Chiefs beat the Broncos, in case you missed that." They regularly bet on football games and the loser had to buy lunch on Monday.

Sam shook his head. "Yeah, yeah, yeah. How about the taco place?"

"You're cheap, but that actually sounds good." She opened the door. "I'll stop back by around noon, okay?"

Sam nodded as he took another gulp of his Diet Coke.

Toni walked out of the courtroom with a grin on her face. The hearing had gone well and the judge decided that the statements and evidence would not be suppressed. The defense attorney had stopped her before she left and asked for a recommendation and plea agreement. That meant she probably wouldn't have to prepare for a trial. Toni told him she'd have the agreement e-mailed to him by this afternoon.

After three detention hearings and six bond hearings, Toni was grateful to return to her office. She grabbed a bottle of water from the refrigerator in the lunchroom before sitting down at her desk. She hadn't even opened the bottle of water when the phone rang.

"There's a Mr. Hamilton on line three for you," Chloe said.

Toni thanked her and grinned. She and Jake Hamilton had been friends since undergrad. He was an architect and had started his own company last year. It was also last year that he finally went public with being gay. Prior to that he'd been rather closeted, fearful that his being gay would prevent him from getting a job at an architectural firm. Now that he had his own firm, he lived with his partner quite openly.

"Hiya, handsome. Are you calling to RSVP for Thanksgiving?"

"No, but I will." He chuckled. "We'll both be there and we're bringing raspberry cheesecake and wine. But that isn't why I called."

"What's up?"

"I'm in the middle of meetings right across the street from you. I was wondering if you could pop over to Phil's Deli around eleven thirty for lunch? My treat."

She glanced at her calendar and saw she was free until two that afternoon. "I'd love to. I'll meet you over there."

He disconnected without saying anything else and she just

smiled. Jake's happiness over the past year was almost contagious. She was anxious to see him and catch up. She looked at her watch and saw that she had about a half hour before lunch. She popped online and looked for Help Services, the shelter that Charlie Jones ran. She found nothing out of the ordinary and it appeared to be just a normal nonprofit shelter with no religious affiliation.

"I believe our waitress is flirting with you," Toni said after their orders had been taken.

Jake rolled his eyes. "Aside from the fact that I'm *so* not interested in girls, she has to be what, twelve years old? Don't you have to be at least sixteen to hold a job? You're a prosecutor, do something."

Toni laughed. "They're getting younger every day. We were at The Cat's Meow a while back and I swear an entire junior high school class came in. Jeez."

"Okay, on to more important things. Don and I are already planning our annual Christmas party, so you might as well pencil in December twenty-second."

Toni and Jake continued talking throughout their meal. The hour passed quickly and Jake had to leave. "I'm sorry I can't stay longer but I've got another meeting," he said. "This has been tons of fun. Next time I'm downtown we have to do this again. And I'm so excited about turkey day. It's going to be fabulous."

They got up to leave and Toni spotted Vicky across the deli. She was sitting at a booth with a man. As they passed by, she and Jake stopped to say hello. Toni introduced Jake, although Vicky already knew him.

"This is Charlie Jones," Vicky said, gesturing to the man across the table.

Toni reached out to shake his hand, as did Jake.

"It's nice to meet you," Jake said. "I hate to be rude, but I'm running late for a meeting." He said goodbye and kissed Toni on the cheek. "See ya later, sweetie."

Toni started to leave.

"Do you have a minute to join us?" Vicky asked.

Toni glanced at her watch. "Sure, I've got a little time." She slid in the booth next to Vicky.

"I was telling Charlie that someone with a van like his was seen in a neighborhood where there have been some reports of a Peeping Tom." She smiled at Toni. "He's been telling me about his shelter."

Toni nodded to Vicky, acknowledging the ruse and turned her attention to Charlie. "What kind of clients do you have there?" Even though she already knew from her research, she didn't want him to know that.

"Mostly schizophrenics and a few bipolar types, but we have some that are dealing with developmental disabilities."

"Toni used to be a psychotherapist before becoming one of our prosecutors," Vicky said. "So she knows what you're talking about."

"That's great," Charlie said, beaming. "We have a day treatment program for the chronic folks and some structured classes for the others. There's also an area that houses the ones that are homeless, as long as they're willing to work."

"What kind of staff do you have?" Toni asked.

"I got my MSW after leaving the department and I run the overall facility. We have four case managers who are all social workers and two master level therapists. We also have a doc that comes in once a week for the meds. What kind of clients did you see?"

"I mostly worked with adolescents," Toni said. "Suicidal, homicidal and the gamut of personality disorders."

"Gee, that's tough work," Charlie said.

"Not nearly as hard as adult chronics," Toni said.

"Do all your staffers have access to the van?" Vicky asked.

Charlie answered while still looking at Toni. "The staff can take the van out at any time. When no one is using it, the keys are hanging on a nail just outside my office."

"Do any of your clients have the ability to drive?" Toni asked.

"Oh, sure. Probably about half of them, but I seriously doubt they could have taken the van without someone else noticing. But you never know."

"Does the van stay at the shelter all the time, or do you take it home with you?" Vicky asked.

"I take it with me a few times a week, I guess," Charlie said. "Maybe more."

Toni noticed that he continued to keep eye contact with her, even though Vicky was the one asking the questions. She smiled at him slightly, trying to keep a mostly neutral expression. This was a skill she'd learned as a therapist and she was very good at not letting people see her emotions or reactions.

"What about the staff?" Vicky asked. "These incidents took place at night. Do you have staff there overnight?"

Charlie glanced at Vicky, then back to Toni. "We always have at least one staff member on the shelter side of the premises. It's usually a case manager. And we do some outpatient therapy in the evenings, so some days there are therapists there until about eight o'clock. I can give you all of the names of all my staff if you think that would help."

"We'd really appreciate that," Toni said.

Charlie took out a pen and paper from his coat pocket and jotted down the names of the six other workers. "Here you go," he said as he handed the paper to Toni. He looked at his watch. "I've got to head back now," he said. "I've got a staff meeting." He placed a ten-dollar bill on the table. "It was really nice meeting you, Ms. Barston. You too, detective. Let me know if there's anything else I can do." He left.

Toni watched him go out the front door before she said anything. She got up and slid into the opposite side of the booth. "Was it just me or did he completely ignore you?"

"I'll say. Holy crap. I mean I know I'm not a beauty queen or anything, but that was really strange. Especially since you're an attorney and all. No offense."

"What do you mean?"

"Well," Vicky said. "Charlie is an old-school cop. It's not like he hates lawyers or anything, but just that they aren't 'us'. And by 'us' I mean cops. Cops stick together. Before you came over to the table, it was like pulling teeth to get him to talk about anything. Usually old cops will talk your ear off about the good old days. Not that he's that old or anything, but still, it was strange."

"Maybe it still bothers him that he had to medically retire," Toni said. "You know, maybe it's a sore spot for him."

"That or he was just flirting with you. He barely looked at me after you arrived."

"I think that was because I used to be a therapist and I knew what he was talking about. That's all." Toni leaned back in the booth and looked at the names on the piece of paper. "Guess you should shoot these over to Patty."

Vicky looked at the names and nodded. "She told me she was going to swing by Johnnie's office to pick up the background info this afternoon." Vicky chuckled. "I don't think that's the only thing she wants to pick up there."

Toni grinned. "Yeah, it was kind of obvious yesterday. I just hope that Johnnie doesn't break her heart."

"Hey, for all we know, Patty is the one who'll be breaking hearts." Vicky placed her own ten-dollar bill on the table and slid out of the booth. She and Toni walked back to Metro together.

# Chapter 12

Toni and Boggs pulled into opposite ends of the alley behind their house at the same time. Toni could see the huge grin on Boggs's face as they both acted like they were about to play chicken. After laughing out loud, Toni hit the garage door opener and pulled in first. Boggs waited until she'd gotten out of her bright blue VW Bug before pulling her SUV into the garage. Toni waited for her by the door to the mudroom.

"We couldn't have timed that any better if we'd planned it," Toni said.

"I know. How strange was that?" Boggs keyed in the code on the security panel on the inside door after the garage door had lowered. They walked through the mudroom, hanging their keys on the pegs near the kitchen door. Toni set her briefcase on the kitchen island next to Mr. Rupert and sighed. She grinned as he pushed his head on her arm.

"Hiya, buddy," she said as she rubbed his head. "I guess you're starving to death. I can almost see your ribs."

Mr. Rupert meowed loudly and blinked at her several times. She retrieved a can of wet food from the cabinet. Before she could finish opening the small can, Little Tuffy jumped up and sat next to his large brother. Mr. Rupert glared at him and Little Tuffy scooted about two feet away. Toni put one third of the can on one plate and the rest on another small plate. She placed the food in front of the boys. It took less than a minute for it to disappear.

Toni shook her head. "It's not like it's been *days* since you two ate," she said, patting each of them. She put their plates into the dishwasher. "You have dry food, you know." Neither seemed to care that she was talking, as their need for her to operate the can opener had passed.

Boggs handed her a cold beer. "Looks like you could use one of these, babe."

Toni took a long drink. "Jeez. I don't think a beer has ever tasted this good. I keep thinking about the killer, and I'm sure we're missing something really obvious, but for the life of me I can't figure out what it is." She set the bottle down on the island. "I'm going to run up and put on my comfies, then I'll fix us something to eat. How does that sound?"

Boggs had already downed half of her own beer. "Let's treat ourselves tonight and order some Chinese food. I don't know about you, but I'm in the mood to be lazy."

Toni picked up her beer and after a long drink, she smiled. "Ah, a woman after my own heart." She took another sip. "Go ahead and order while I change."

By the time Toni returned downstairs, Boggs was sitting in the living room, drinking what appeared to be her second beer. Her legs were stretched out on the ottoman.

"You must have had one hell of a day yourself," Toni said as she grabbed her own beer from the kitchen island. She plopped down in the other leather club chair. Mr. Rupert hopped up on her lap. "What happened?"

Boggs was absentmindedly scratching Little Tuffy, who was curled up in her lap. "It was just one of those days where I couldn't get anything done. Interviews where the guy doesn't show up or where the woman conveniently forgets what happened in a robbery. Like you could forget if there were one, two or three guys who supposedly held a gun to your head. She changes her story every time I talk to her. We already know her boyfriend was one of the perps, but she's adamantly denying that. Drives me crazy. I'm having an 'I hate people' kind of day." She took another swallow of beer. "And I've been doing some digging on Peter. Sam gave me his personnel file. Or at least Sam's version of that."

"Sorry about your lousy interviews. Did you find anything on Peter?"

"Nope, not really, but I just started. He just gives me the creeps. I did find out he's a Republican."

Toni laughed. "Well, that's enough to make me question his sanity."

"I just wish there was something I could put my finger on," Boggs said. "But so far there isn't. It's bugging me."

"Maybe he just gives off a bad vibe," Toni said. "You know, icky energy or something? I've only worked with him a few times and that's what I pick up from him."

"You might have something there. At first, I thought it was just a personality clash between us or something, but now I think you may be right. Vicky can't stand him either, and Sam said he'd fire him if he had a good reason." Boggs finished her beer and set the empty bottle on the end table. She glanced at her watch. "The food should be here any minute. I ordered extra so we could have leftovers for lunch and such."

"Yum." Toni finished her own beer and went to get them both replacements. The doorbell rang just as she was putting the bottles in the recycle bin. She glanced at the monitor on the kitchen counter and saw it was the regular boy from Dragon Inn. She grabbed some cash from her wallet in her briefcase and paid for their food. The brown bag was huge.

"Holy crap, hon, were you hungry or something?"

Boggs came over and started to unload the food while Toni got out plates, bowls and flatware.

"I couldn't decide between cashew chicken or shrimp with snow peas," she said, grinning. "And I didn't know if you wanted beef with broccoli or chicken and snow peas, so I got one of each. And I also got us egg rolls and soup with an extra order of fried rice for lunch tomorrow."

Toni smiled as she watched Boggs pull out each container. She looked like a kid at Christmas, examining each and every present. Toni kissed her on the cheek before sitting at the island.

As they ate and sampled each other's food, Toni filled her in on the meeting with Charlie Jones.

"I agree with Vicky," Boggs said after swallowing another bite. "I think he was hitting on you."

"No, I don't think so," Toni said. "I mean it's possible of course, but I didn't get that vibe. Not at all."

"Well, the strangest thing was the fact that he didn't bore Vicky to death with old cop stories. She's right. I've never met a retired cop that didn't tell an assload of stories or at least give you advice about how to investigate something." Boggs took a sip of her third beer. "But maybe he's just an odd one, like Peter."

"You're probably right. I mean, well, he was very upfront about the people at his shelter and the workers. Patty will run those names for us." Toni pushed her plate away. "I am stuffed. And it looks like we barely touched all the food here."

Boggs finished the last of her egg roll and started to put the food away.

"I'll do that for us, honey," Toni said as she pushed her stool back from the island.

"No, that's okay, babe. I've got it. Why don't you stay there and let's go over our Thanksgiving list while I clean up?"

Toni nodded and smiled. She got the list out of the island drawer and sat back down. She watched Boggs move about the kitchen with ease, putting dishes in the dishwasher and putting the food into containers for the refrigerator. She couldn't believe how incredibly lucky she was. She lived in this beautiful home with her partner and best friend. They'd just treated themselves to Chinese food and now they were planning a family holiday.

She saw Mr. Rupert sleeping on the couch in the living room and Little Tuffy was curled up on one of the ottomans. Toni felt loved and safe, and tears began to well up in her eyes.

She blinked several times, trying to keep her emotions in check, but the tears wouldn't cooperate. What had she done to deserve such a wonderful life? The thought of losing everything at the hands of a delusional maniac, just like Maggie had, was too much for her to comprehend.

Boggs had just put the last plate in the dishwasher when she noticed a very emotional Toni, tears streaming down her face. "Are you okay, babe?" She quickly crossed the room and wrapped her arms around Toni. "What's wrong?" Toni saw her gaze dart around the room as though she were looking for the source of her anguish.

"I just love you so much," Toni whispered. "I can't bear the thought of not having you."

Boggs visibly relaxed, kissing her cheek and wiping away the tears with her sleeve. "You're not going to lose me, babe. Not if I have anything to say about it." She pulled Toni off the barstool and held her close. "We're okay," she whispered in Toni's ear. "We're okay."

"I'm sorry, hon," Toni said. "I don't know what got into me."

"It's fine, babe. I felt that way just a few months ago when I thought that woman had killed you. It just washed over me and I couldn't stop the tears." Boggs lightly touched Toni's cheek, then kissed her. "How about I fix us a cup of coffee and we just relax in front of the fire for a bit?"

"That sounds wonderful." Toni took a deep breath, then hugged Boggs one more time. "In fact, if you make the coffee, I'll put some frozen apple turnovers in the oven. How does that sound?"

"Like a perfect night."

Toni was able to push past that emotional overload, and by the time the turnovers were ready to come out of the oven, she and Boggs were laughing at the antics of Mr. Rupert and Little Tuffy. They spent the rest of the evening curled up on the couch with the fire roaring and football on their flat screen television.

He had spent the last hour in his sanctuary, praying and going over his new list. He felt more inspired than he'd ever felt before. On his way home from work that evening, he'd seen a billboard. Even though he usually drove the same route, he'd never seen that sign before. There was no doubt in his mind that this was a sign from God. It was an advertisement for a local restaurant.

## CHANGE YOUR ROUTINE—ADD US TO YOUR "TO DO" LIST
### EAT AT JENNY'S RESTAURANT TONIGHT!

He knew that this message was meant for him and only him. He had been given permission to expand his mission. He twisted his ring. This was better than he could hope for. He knew that soon everyone would know about him and praise his work. As he pulled up in front of his house, another message came through a song on the radio. He was so excited that God was now communicating with him not only through his dreams and meditation, but also through the media and no one but he could understand. He was special.

After thirty minutes of prayer and extensive research on his laptop, he decided that not only would he give his regular sermon tonight, he'd add someone new. He felt almost giddy. He also decided that he needed to change his technique for getting into these people's homes. The message from God on the billboard was not only a gift, allowing him to cast out more deviants, but also a warning that he needed to change his routine. It was wonderful.

With a new method set in his mind, he grabbed his gym bag and went downstairs. His mother was in her faded green recliner watching television. She looked puzzled when she saw his bag.

"Where are you going? Tonight isn't your gym night." She seemed confused.

"I know, Mother. But with the holidays coming up, I want to

make sure I don't gain any weight." He smiled. "Especially with all the wonderful goodies that you make this time of year."

She grinned. "I've got a list of things I'll need from the grocery store soon," she said.

"I can get them tonight if you'd like," he said. "Or I can take you to the store after I come home tomorrow. Whichever you prefer."

She thought for a moment. "If it wouldn't be too much trouble, I'd like to go with you tomorrow. I like to see what they have."

"I'll make sure I go to the gym early tomorrow, and that way I'll be home before dinner. We can go to the store right after that." He kissed her on the cheek. "Okay. I'll be back soon."

He had to make himself walk calmly out the door. He was so excited about his expanding mission for God. Tonight would be one on God's list, and Wednesday would be one of his own choosing. He'd have to wait a day since he promised to take his mother to the grocery store, but that was fine. *Honor your mother and father.*

# Chapter 13

Toni had just sat at her desk on Tuesday morning when Vicky called. There'd been an attempt last night. *What went wrong?* Toni chided herself. *Maybe I should be thinking, what went right?*

"I'm guessing that this woman's neighbor scared our guy off," Vicky said. "The victim is still unconscious and Claire said she'd call as soon as she knows anything. She thinks he only got a partial dose of the insulin in before the neighbor started pounding on the door."

"Did the neighbor see anything?" Toni asked. "Was that why the neighbor was so persistent?"

"She didn't see a damn thing," Vicky said. "She was having a crisis of her own. She's a bit of a drama queen. But I want to talk to everyone in the neighborhood after I finish in here. I think I'll be here at the scene for another hour or so. We've been here all night. Patty is doing some interviews right now and I've already called Johnnie."

"Are you sure it's the same as the others?" Toni asked.

"As far as I can tell, yes. I was hoping he'd make a mistake and maybe this is it. I hope I'm not just missing something."

"I keep feeling that way," Toni said. "Like there's something obvious that I'm not seeing." She took a deep breath. "Why don't you all come over around six and maybe we can sort this out?"

"Sounds good." She rang off without saying anything else.

Toni frowned as she replaced the phone. *What can I do?* Someone needs to look into that shelter, she thought. The clients, not just the staff. But with privacy concerns, she wasn't sure how to do that. Since Charlie seemed very friendly to her, she decided to give him a call. It couldn't hurt to try. She looked up the number and called immediately.

"Hi, Charlie. It's Toni Barston. I met you yesterday with Detective Carter?"

"Oh, sure, Ms. Barston. How are you?"

"I'm doing good, thanks. But please, call me Toni. I wanted to talk to you about your clients. I'm concerned about this Peeping Tom, and I wondered if you had any ideas or concerns about any of them. I'm afraid he might escalate." Toni hoped this ruse would work. It was worth a shot.

"I thought about that last night," Charlie said. "And there might be two or three." He hesitated for a moment. "I can't really violate confidentiality you know," he continued, "but if you came over for a tour, I may be able to introduce you to some of our clients."

Toni quickly looked at her appointment book and saw that she was free from noon until two. "Would it be okay if I came over around twelve thirty?"

"That would be great," Charlie said. "I can show you around the facility and the folks I'd like you to meet will be here. I'll see you soon."

"Thank you. I'll see you later."

Toni called Boggs to fill her in.

"Just be careful," Boggs said. "Make sure you're never alone with any of the crazy people."

Toni laughed. "I think I can handle it, hon. I'll call you when

I get back to the office, okay?"

"Okay. Once you've got the names from Charlie, let Vicky know so she can do a background check on them. Maybe she can have the info by the time they come over tonight. Oh, what are we doing for food?"

"I didn't even think about that," Toni said. "Any ideas?"

"I think Chinese is out," Boggs said, chuckling. "I ate it for breakfast and I'm planning on eating it for lunch."

"How does spaghetti sound?" Toni tried to think of something warm and comforting, but easy to fix.

"Oh, wow. That sounds fabulous, but you don't have time, do you?"

Toni was well known for her spaghetti and meatballs made from scratch. It took about three hours to make a batch and she only knew how to make a massive amount. It was her mother's recipe that had taken years to perfect. The recipe card just listed ingredients, no amounts, so she was never really sure how each batch would turn out. After she made the huge pot, she usually froze the rest in small portions, just enough for her and Boggs.

"I can stop by the house on the way to the shelter and take it out of the freezer. I'm pretty sure there are three containers in there and that should be enough for the five of us, don't you think? Then on my way home from work I'll stop and get fresh salad stuff and bread."

"That sounds *so* good," Boggs said. "That should be enough for all of us. But, I'll stop at the store, babe. Do you want sweet bread or garlic bread?"

"Oh, sweetie, that's perfect. Thank you. And it doesn't matter which bread you get. Whatever sounds good to you." Toni thought for a moment. "I know that Vicky loves my spaghetti, but what about Patty and Johnnie? Not everyone likes sweet spaghetti sauce."

"Don't worry about it, babe. But I'll call them to make sure," Boggs offered. "And I'm positive they will. If they don't they can always fill up on bread and beer."

"Very funny, but okay. That sounds like a plan." Toni was

a little nervous about having Patty and Johnnie try her sauce for the first time. *What if they hate it? And they sit there hungry?* She laughed when she realized the absurdity of what she was thinking. There was a maniac wandering around Fairfield and she was worried about someone not liking her cooking? Now who's crazy? "I'll call you when I get back to the office," she said to Boggs. "I love you."

"I love you, too, babe. And be careful," Boggs cautioned.

Toni spent the rest of the morning working on research for an upcoming suppression hearing. As always when she was doing research, the time got away from her. She literally jumped when the phone buzzed.

"Your mom is on line four, Ms. Barston," Chloe said.

Toni glanced at her watch before pushing the button. It was already eleven thirty. "I'm so glad you called, Mom. I completely lost track of time. What's up?"

"I'm working on lemon bars today," her mom announced, not even saying hello. "And I just wanted to know what kind of dessert you want us to bring for Thanksgiving so I can make sure I've got that kind done already."

Toni's mom began her holiday baking on November first every year. She would bake one type of goodie each day, all day, until the middle of December. Then she and Toni's dad would take boxes and put in two or three of each treat to give as gifts. Everything was made from scratch and was absolutely wonderful. Lemon bars were one of Toni's favorites.

"I'd love for you to bring a cherry pie, of course," Toni said. It was another one of her mom's specialties. "And maybe just a small assortment of whatever you've made so far? How would that be? I don't want you to do too much."

"It's no trouble at all," her mom insisted. "Your dad and I are making a little extra this year of everything. Are you sure I can't bring a hot dish? I think you'll need another veggie, so I'll bring that green bean casserole that everyone likes. And a relish tray. Oh, and your dad wants pecan pie, so I'll bring that."

"Mom!" Toni interrupted. "You don't have to bring all that."

"Oh, it's just a few things. Are you sure you'll have enough? This is your first time having Thanksgiving you know."

"Yes, I know, and I'm pretty sure we'll have enough," Toni said. "We have a twenty-two pound turkey that I'll roast on Thanksgiving Day and a twenty pound one that I'll fix the day before. We also have a huge ham and I'm making a double batch of broccoli-rice casserole. Boggs is in charge of the mashed potatoes and gravy. Oh, she's also making cauliflower surprise casserole."

"That's not enough," her mom insisted.

"And everyone who is coming is bringing something, so we'll be fine," Toni said.

"As long as you're sure," her mom said. "But I'm going to bring the ingredients to make the stuffing. Just because you don't like it doesn't mean we shouldn't have it. And maybe dressing also. Since you have that wonderful double oven, I'm bringing the ingredients to make oyster dressing." Her mother seemed to be thinking out loud. "Okay, I have to get back to baking. I'll talk to you soon. Love you."

Toni grinned. "I love you, too, Mom. Tell Dad I said howdy and not to eat all the peanut clusters."

Her mom was laughing as she hung up.

Toni had just enough time to heat up some leftover fried rice in the lunchroom before heading out. She stopped at home and was relieved to find three containers of spaghetti sauce in the freezer. She set them on the counter and Mr. Rupert appeared at her feet.

"Hiya, buddy. Just getting out food for dinner."

He jumped up to investigate, pushing one of the containers with his head.

"Don't you dare push that off the counter, young man." She moved the frozen sauce to the back. "How about a Scooby snack to take your mind off of this?" She got some cat treats out of the drawer and made a small pile for him. She took a few more and put them on the island for Little Tuffy. "I expect to see the sauce exactly where I left it when I get home," she said to the boys. "If

96

not, you're both grounded. Mr. Rupert, you are in charge." She rubbed his head before heading back to her car.

Toni pulled into the parking lot of Help Services at exactly twelve thirty. Charlie was standing next to the receptionist's desk when she walked inside. She strode across the waiting room and extended her hand. "Good to see you again, Charlie."

Charlie shook her hand, smiling. She felt herself bristle at his touch. *What's that about?* She shook off the feeling and concentrated on her task.

"Nice to see you," Charlie said. "I'd like you to meet Clara, our receptionist."

Toni turned and shook her hand. "Very nice to meet you." She looked back to Charlie. "Thanks for giving me a tour of your center."

He nodded. "Absolutely. Of course the catch is that you'll like what you see and donate at one of our fundraisers."

"Sounds fair to me," Toni said. She gave a small wave to Clara, who was now on the phone, as Charlie led her to his office. He gave her a general description of the services they provided on the way. Once inside, he pointed to an empty chair before taking a seat behind his desk.

"As you know," he began, "I can't violate the confidentiality of our clients here. But since I used to be a cop, I understand your concern. Those guys who look in windows are disgusting, and I hope you catch the son of a bitch. There was a guy on the west side that we were after for almost a year. We didn't catch him until he actually broke into a house and assaulted a young woman. It made me sick, but we got him."

Toni listened as Charlie told one story after another. *Why didn't he do this with Vicky, and why is he giving me the creeps?* After nearly thirty minutes, she took the opportunity to stop him. "I'm so glad you understand our predicament, Charlie. Could you show me around and introduce me to some of your clients? Maybe you could just give me the full names of a few, if that's okay with you?"

Charlie grinned. "Good idea. Some of the guys I'll just

introduce you and tell you their first name. Perfect."

Most of the clients were working in the kitchen area, cleaning up after lunch. A few were relaxing in the game room. After the complete tour, Toni had three names. When Charlie had given her the full name of a man, she made sure she talked to him for at least five minutes, trying to get an idea of his personality. Back in Charlie's office, she jotted down the names, making sure she had the correct spelling. "Thank you so much, Charlie. And let me know when your next fundraiser will be."

"Sure, my pleasure. Maybe you and your husband can come to one of our trivia nights."

"Oh, I'm not married," she said. Toni saw a flicker of confusion on Charlie's face and his smile disappeared. It took her only a moment to understand, and a moment longer to confirm her suspicion as she glanced around his office.

"Jake and I are very close," she confided to Charlie in a whisper. She saw the smile return to his face. "And I'm very hopeful." She gave him a smile and glanced at her watch. "Oh, I've got to get back to the office. Thanks again for all your help." She debated her next move for just a moment. "And here's my card in case you think of anything that might be helpful. Call me anytime."

Charlie took the card and nodded. "I hope you find the guy. And here's a flyer about our trivia night. I hope to see you and Jake there."

Toni took the flyer, thanked him again and headed back to her car. "Well, that clears a few things up," she muttered to herself as she drove out of the lot. She called Vicky and gave her the names, telling her she'd fill her in tonight. She left the same message for Boggs. Toni was still mumbling to herself and shaking her head when she pulled into the parking garage at Metro.

She barely had enough time to get the files out of her office before literally running to the courtroom for several detention hearings. Only one of those was seriously contested and she spent well over twenty minutes arguing back and forth with the defense attorney. The judge finally ruled in her favor and she was able to make it back to her office by three o'clock.

It was nearly four thirty when she finished the paperwork she had piled on her desk. She checked her calendar for tomorrow and got a few things ready before heading home.

She was warming the spaghetti and meatballs on the stove when Boggs came home. She kissed Toni, then unloaded three loaves of bread and pre-made salad from the reusable grocery bag. Toni handed her a beer from the fridge.

"Thanks, babe." She took several gulps. "Your message said you figured out Charlie. What's up?"

"He's an ass," Toni said matter-of-factly after taking a sip of Boggs's beer. "Run up and change and I'll fill you in once the others are here."

"I see we're dressing up for company," Boggs said, grinning.

Toni was wearing red plaid flannel sleep pants, a red Chiefs sweatshirt and red moccasin type slippers. "Yes. I think it's very important to make a good impression on guests." She laughed. "Don't you like my outfit?"

"I think you look adorable." Boggs wrapped her arms around Toni and kissed her passionately. "I wish they weren't coming over," she whispered.

Toni leaned back, but then pulled her girl close and hugged her. "I love how much we love each other. We'll kick them out early, okay?"

Boggs nodded and returned a few minutes later wearing an Air Force sweatshirt, sweatpants and white fuzzy slippers. She pointed to her ensemble and Toni grinned.

Boggs had just finished putting out placemats and plates on the kitchen island when the doorbell rang. Looking at the security monitor, they both saw Vicky waving at them, holding up a six-pack of beer.

"I guess we should let her in," Toni said.

Johnnie and Patty were walking up the sidewalk as Toni opened the front door. "Dinner will be ready in just a minute. Come on in, you guys."

They hung their coats on the pegs in the foyer and followed

Toni into the kitchen.

"Wow," Patty said. "That smells wonderful."

"I sure hope you like it," Toni said. "Not everyone likes sweet sauce."

"Nice slippers, Boggs." Johnnie snickered.

Boggs ignored her. She had just finished slicing the bread and dipped a piece in the sauce. She handed it to Patty. "Here. See what you think."

Patty blew on the bread and took a small bite. It took only a moment before her eyes got big. "Yum!" She tore off the other end of her bread and dipped it in again. This time she handed the bread to Johnnie.

"Damn, Toni," Johnnie said while still chewing. "That's the best I've ever tasted."

"I'm so glad. Sit down, everyone." She took their drink orders and gave each one a beer, then put the pasta on to boil. Boggs took care of the salad.

After they had stuffed themselves with meatballs, salad and bread, Toni gave them fresh drinks and sent them to the basement. She felt so good that they had all enjoyed her spaghetti. She only wished that the reason for the gathering was something other than tracking a serial killer. She put the plates in the dishwasher and left the rest to deal with later. Grabbing herself another beer from the fridge, she headed downstairs to join the others.

"So what did you find out about Charlie?" Vicky asked as soon as she sat. "Then I'll fill you all in on what I know."

"He's a homophobe," Toni said. "And an ass. He gives me the creeps. He thought I was married to Jake and when I said I wasn't, his whole attitude changed. It was almost comical if it weren't so pathetic. I noticed a bunch of religious stuff in his office, so I decided to play it straight and he instantly came back around. I'm positive that's why he hardly spoke to you, Vicky. It's no secret that you're out."

Vicky nodded. "Makes sense to me. What an asshole."

"Why would he think you're married to Jake?" Johnnie asked.

"I guess because he saw us together at Phil's Deli yesterday," Toni said. "We stopped by the booth and I introduced him to Charlie. I guess he just assumed."

"So, did he tell you old war stories?" Vicky asked.

"Sure did. Just like you guys described. And he gave me all kinds of advice on how to catch our Peeping Tom."

"Peeping Tom?" Patty looked confused.

"We told him that's why we were looking at his van," Vicky said. "It was seen near where a Peeping Tom was bothering women."

"So with this ruse, I think I'm the best go-between with Charlie," Toni said. "Unfortunately, he's more likely to cooperate if he thinks I'm straight. I don't like to pretend, but as long as we need his help, so be it." She sighed. "So what about last night's attempt?" she asked. "Same thing? And how is she doing?"

"As far as we can tell," Vicky said, "it's the same. Her name is Amy Judge and she works at that little hardware store near Peach Tree Park. She lives alone in a small duplex. The woman who lives on the other side came over and pounded on the door. She didn't hear a thing from Amy's side, but she was having a huge fight with her boyfriend and *needed* to talk to Amy immediately. Apparently, she does this all the time. Anyway, she knew Amy was in there and after pounding for a few seconds, she let herself in with her key. Amy was duct taped to the kitchen chair and was unconscious. The syringe was on the floor and the back door was wide open. Unfortunately, no one saw anything."

"Is she still unconscious?" Toni asked.

"Yes," Vicky replied. "I talked to Claire just before I got here, and there's been no change. She's in a coma from the insulin. The first twenty-four hours are the most critical, and if she does wake up, she could have cognitive, neurological and emotional problems."

Toni shook her head. "How the hell is he finding these people?" She set her beer on the coffee table and began pacing around the room. "He must have a list or a specific pool of victims. At least in his head." She rounded the pool table. "But what kind of list is it and where is he coming up with the names? It's not like we have a registry or something."

"You mean like the *Gay Yellow Pages*?" Patty asked.

"We sure as hell aren't *listed*," Boggs said. "And yet this guy has killed three people who were either gay or the parent of a gay and almost killed another. You're right, Toni. Where's he getting his information?"

"Even the FBI doesn't have a list like that," Johnnie added.

Toni continued to walk around the room. "Lists. Lists. Lists." She stopped dead in her tracks. "How many of you are members of the Fairfield Human Rights Campaign? You know, signed up at Pridefest to get a free T-shirt?"

Everyone in the room slowly raised her hand.

Toni shrugged. "Worth a shot, don't you think? Can you get a copy of their roster or whatever?" she asked Vicky.

"Legally, I'd need a subpoena," Vicky said as she pulled out her phone. "But lucky for us, I used to date the treasurer."

"Who haven't you dated?" Johnnie snickered.

Vicky flipped her off and went over to the pinball machine for some privacy. Toni returned to her spot on the couch.

Ten minutes later Vicky rejoined the group. "She's e-mailing me the list now."

"Let's go up to the study so you can print it out," Boggs said.

They came back down with several copies and handed them out. Patty was the first one to finish scanning the list. "Yup, you were right. All of them are on this list." She took a long drink of her beer. "And so are we. Except for you, Toni. How come?"

"I'm not?" She thought for a moment. "Oh, I guess I was a bit of a mess at Pride last summer, remember?" She laughed. She'd gone undercover that day and never had a chance to stop at all the booths. "And I guess I didn't renew this fall. Probably because we moved and I didn't get the notice. I suppose the T-shirt I've been wearing belongs to Boggs." She looked at her copy of the list. "But there are at least two hundred names here. How is he picking?"

"And how the hell did he get this list, if that's what he's got?" Johnnie asked.

Vicky thought for a moment. "You know, I think just about anyone could get this. I didn't even have to go into a long, drawn-out reason with Susie. I just said I was working on something and could I have the membership list. Maybe it's public information."

"Well, that's pretty scary," Toni said. "But I bet it's probably like most businesses and they sell their client lists, or share with other nonprofit organizations. That's how we get so much junk mail, or I guess spam now."

"You're probably right," Boggs said. "I don't remember seeing anything when we signed up that said our identity was protected. Usually if that's true they make a huge deal out of it."

"Okay, so let's say our guy got a copy of this list, or some kind of list. Doesn't matter," Vicky said. "We still don't know how he's picking out of that list and in what order. We need to go back to basics and see what we already know."

"Did you run the names I gave you from the shelter?" Toni asked.

"Yup." Vicky sat her beer on the coffee table and dug in her backpack. She pulled out a notepad and flipped through the pages. "Okay, the first guy is Frank Watson. He has a prior for flashing some woman at a mall. I looked at the police report, and apparently, he's a bit challenged intellectually. I don't think he could plan a picnic, let alone these killings."

"Yeah," Toni said. "I didn't get the feeling he was our guy when I met him."

"You met these crazy people?" Johnnie seemed alarmed.

"Sure. Charlie gave me a tour of the place. It was pretty much the same kind of place I worked as a psychotherapist. I talked for a bit to all three of these guys, just so I could get an idea of who they were. Only a first impression, though."

Johnnie lit a cigarette. "Gives me the creeps, that's all."

Vicky made a face at Johnnie and flipped to the next page of her pad. "Okay, the second guy is Mevin Murran and he has three priors. One is an assault and the other two are DWIs."

"Did you say Mevin Murran?" Patty asked.

"Yeah, isn't that a hoot?" Vicky said.

"Who in their right mind names their kid Mevin?" Boggs said.

"If you could have seen him, you'd have understood," Toni said. "He's not right, and I got a bad vibe from him. He seemed very paranoid to me, but I have no idea of his diagnosis. He's the one that I would have picked out of all the guys that I saw. And there's something else."

"What?" Boggs asked. "Did he do something to you?"

Toni thought Boggs was ready to grab her gun and go after this guy. She smiled. It was so nice knowing that Boggs, and the rest of them for that matter, would protect her if they could. "No. He didn't *do* anything. He's very handsome." She paused a moment. "His look is intense, almost alluring."

"And what?" Johnnie asked. "You're thinking of dating him?"

"Incredibly funny," Toni replied. "No, it just made me think of Ted Bundy. He was a good-looking guy who could charm women. Unfortunately, he also killed them. But maybe this is the way our killer is getting into homes."

"That might have worked on John," Vicky said. "He was gay. But what about Maggie? And now Amy?"

"I didn't mean it necessarily like that," Toni said. "But our killer might be charming or charismatic. There's got to be something about him that gets him in the front door. We need to think about how this guy gets inside. What's his ruse?"

"That makes sense to me," Boggs said. The others agreed.

"Something to consider when we're looking at people," Vicky said. "Especially the crazy people like Mevin."

"Can't we ask Charlie what his diagnosis is?" Patty asked. "Maybe that would help Toni figure him out."

"No," Toni shook her head. "Confidentiality. But here's an idea. If he's got priors, maybe there's something in the court records. Sometimes the defense counsel will file a psychological report in an attempt to get a lower sentence. It's worth a shot. I'll take a look tomorrow."

"What about the third guy?" Boggs asked.

"Winner number three is Robert Cook," Vicky said. "He has two priors for car theft. And a butt-load of juvenile convictions. What kind of vibe did you get from him, Toni?"

"He seemed like a follower, not a leader to me. As though he was looking for acceptance and approval from the other guys there at the shelter. I don't think it's him."

"So that leaves us with Mevin." Johnnie snickered. "Give us the details."

Vicky flipped back to that page. "Okay, he's forty-two years old. He got his DWIs about a year ago."

"What was the assault?" Boggs asked. "What did he do?"

"He got into a fight at a bar," Vicky said. "And apparently beat the ever-loving shit out of some guy in there."

"Anything to indicate that maybe the guy was gay or something?" Toni asked.

"Nothing in the record that I could find."

"I say we leave him in," Boggs said. "Maybe check with the cop who wrote the report and see if there's anything that he didn't write down."

"Agreed." Vicky pulled out a different notepad. "Okay, on this last attempt by the maniac, there were no prints anywhere. Not even on the syringe. And no forced entry. Oh, and I got the results back from Maggie's laptop. Nothing unusual there, and she apparently never went into chat rooms or anything. Basically, all of the forensics came up empty."

"Why don't we call Cathy and see if she can tell us anything?" Toni said. "Can't hurt to give that a shot." Cathy was a friend of Patty's sister and was a gifted psychic. She'd helped them in a couple of cases over the past year.

Patty was already dialing her phone. After giving Cathy a brief description of what was going on, Patty snapped her phone shut. She was smiling. "She's on her way over now."

"Fantastic," Toni said. "Who wants a fresh beer?"

Fifteen minutes later Cathy was sitting in the basement with them. Patty started to fill her in on the details.

"No, don't give me any more information," Cathy said, interrupting her. "Let me see what I get without that."

"Would it help if you had something he touched?" Vicky asked.

"Hell, yes," Cathy said.

"I've got one of the Bibles he left," Vicky said. "There wasn't any trace evidence on it, so we can touch it. It's in my car. I'll be right back."

"I'll buzz you back in," Boggs said. She went behind the bar to stand next to the monitor.

Vicky returned with a plastic evidence bag. She looked at Johnnie. "Got a pocketknife?"

Johnnie tossed her a small Swiss Army knife and Vicky carefully cut a new opening in the plastic and slid out the Bible. She handed it to Cathy.

Cathy held the Bible and sat quietly for several minutes. You could have heard a pin drop. Even Mr. Rupert waited and watched quietly. Slowly, Cathy opened her eyes. "This is a very disturbed man," she said softly. "Definitely a man. And he's doing what he's doing for God. At least he thinks so."

"Great," Johnnie mumbled.

"I can tell there was a huge change about a year ago," Cathy continued. "And that he has a list, maybe two lists, that he's following." She shook her head. "And there's something about jewelry, like he plays with it or fiddles with it. I don't know if it's a ring or a watch, but something like that. I'm not getting anything else, sorry." She handed the Bible back to Vicky.

With the Bible back inside the evidence bag, Vicky pulled a new evidence seal from her bag and closed the opening. She scribbled her initials over the seal and dropped it in her backpack.

"That was great information," Toni said to Patty. "Thank you. I think this will help us quite a bit, and it confirms some of our theories. Now, how about a drink?"

"Oh, I'd love to, but I've got another appointment. Your place was on my way. I'm sorry I can't stay longer." Cathy seemed disappointed.

"We just appreciate that you could make it," Toni said. "Here, let me walk you back up." She headed upstairs with Cathy.

When she returned, Patty and Johnnie had their laptops open on the bar. "Okay, let's see what we have so far," Toni said. "And see if anything fits with what Cathy said, especially the part about something happening or changing in this guy's life a year ago."

"I ran all the workers at Help Services," Patty said. "And I got squat. We've got a total of six people aside from Charlie, and five are women."

"I think we can skip them," Johnnie said.

"Okay, well that leaves one guy." Patty pushed her laptop to the side and pulled out a notepad from her bag. "His name is Ryan Hollinger and he's one of the therapists. He's also a professor at the university. No priors. He's married and has two kids. And I found out he was giving a lecture in St. Louis on the night of the last murder, but I don't know about any other dates."

"Guess that pretty much eliminates him," Vicky said. "Okay, let's go back to our original people. I think we have four good suspects," Vicky said. "Let's combine our information and see if there's anyone we can eliminate."

Johnnie hit a few keys on her laptop. "I ran background checks on our main suspects, except the new guy, Mevin. I'll do him now." She typed in a few more lines. "He's forty-two years old, like Vicky said." She continued typing. "Looks like he used to be a nurse, but his license was yanked after those DWIs. Last year's tax return shows that he worked at Christian Hospital as an orderly, part-time. And like you saw, Toni, he works part-time at the shelter and gets outpatient therapy there. Looks like he's having a hard time getting his life back together."

"Jeez," Toni said. "That would give him access to insulin at the hospital now and the medical knowledge. And the DWIs were a year ago. He seems to fit the bill. I wonder if we can find out what happened to him then."

"He's definitely at the top of my list," Vicky said.

"Next is weird neighbor Joe Jackson," Johnnie continued. "No priors, as Patty already told us. He's been at the county library for eighteen years. He's forty years old and has been a registered Republican since he was eighteen."

"Figures," Boggs added.

"He's also a member of the National Rifle Association. No credit problems, but he did have some issues with the IRS about a year ago."

"That keeps him on the list in my book," Patty said.

Johnnie hit more keys. "Next is David Davidson. He's forty-seven years old and has had at least twelve jobs in sales. This last one for the pharmaceutical company has lasted for a little over a year. He's pretty much off the radar. No affiliations, and he's not even registered to vote."

"Been at the job for just over a year," Toni said. "Maybe that's significant. Something could have happened a year ago like Cathy said. Same as Joe."

"Good point," Vicky said. "He definitely stays on the list. Plus, just the fact that his parents named him David Davidson. He's probably got issues." She laughed at her own wit.

"And then there's your favorite, Boggs, Peter Johnson." Johnnie grinned.

"Did he make it on the asshole meter?" Boggs asked.

"Pretty much," Johnnie said. "He's also a Republican and he belongs to some group called *The Fellowship*."

"What the hell is that?" Boggs asked.

"It's a religious organization," Johnnie explained. "He joined when he was in college, and it's basically a Christian men's group. They don't do much, at least not as far as the FBI is concerned. As far as jobs go, it looks like he actually worked for this organization for several years after college. But he didn't get paid much according to his tax returns. And it looks like he spent a couple years doing mission work."

"What does that mean?" Patty asked.

"I'm not really sure," Johnnie said. "I think it's similar to

Mormons when the boys do a two-year mission. The only thing I can tell from the IRS files is that he received a stipend from the church during those years. After that, he started working for the Texas park system as a guide I think."

"He was a state park ranger in Texas right before he came to work at Metro," Boggs added. "He did a few investigations into arson and vandalism."

"Why did he move up here to Fairfield?" Toni asked. "Any idea?"

"He told Sam that he'd gotten a divorce," Boggs said. "But I ran a check in Texas and not only did I *not* find any divorce records, I didn't find any marriage license. And he only worked as a park ranger for about two years."

"So what's he hiding?" Vicky asked.

"No clue. Here's the weirdest thing. In the file that Sam gave me, there's no other employment listed besides the park ranger stuff."

"So how the hell did he get the job?" Toni asked.

"A letter of recommendation from the mayor, that's how," Boggs said, shaking her head.

"How much you want to bet the mayor is also a member of The Fellowship?" Johnnie said. "Let me see if I can get anything on our lovely mayor." She hit several keys. "I'm only doing a quick search here," she said as she kept typing. After a couple minutes she leaned back and lit a cigarette. "Yup. Mayor Planscot is a member of The Fellowship. Guess that's how Mr. Creepy got his job as an investigator at Metro."

"That makes me sick," Boggs said as she got up from the couch. "It's one thing if you're qualified and you know someone to help you get a job. But Peter's degree is in forestry and he only had a tiny bit of experience in investigations." She held up her beer. "Anyone ready for a refill?" Everyone nodded and she retrieved the beer from the refrigerator behind the bar. After taking several gulps, she sat back down next to Toni on the couch. "You know, like I said, I wouldn't have minded so much if he'd had a good background with relevant experience. But only two years? And a few minor investigations? There were a lot of good applicants when he applied. I bet it really pissed off Sam that the mayor pushed for this guy."

"I want to know what he's hiding," Vicky said. "Even if you have a sure thing recommendation from the mayor, you would at least list your employment history, wouldn't you? Why didn't he put the park guide stuff in there and his mission crap? He could have easily fluffed it up a bit to make it look decent. But by leaving it off completely, that makes me very suspicious."

"I'd think so, yes," Toni said. "And we all have to go through a background check, so how did he manage that? Did the mayor just fast-track him? Skip all the normal preliminaries?"

"I'm going to look into this guy really hard," Johnnie said. "Even if he's not our killer, which I'm kind of thinking he is, I think this is a bunch of crap. I'm also going to look into Mayor Planscot just a bit." She grinned.

"I did a little bit of digging on him a few months ago," Vicky said. "Remember all that crap about the dirty judges? The ones that liked prostitutes or little boys? Anne Mulhoney had me look into everyone that could have had a hand in that stuff. The mayor was always on the fringe. I never got anything solid on him, but now it makes me wonder."

"You know what I think?" Boggs was obviously angry. "I think our piece of shit mayor is covering up for Peter. How much do you want to bet he's been in trouble before and this so-called organization is helping? Makes me think of the Catholic Church covering up for the priests who abused kids. Plus there's the Bible angle here."

Toni squeezed Boggs's arm. "You might be right, but then again he may *just* be a total sleaze ball," she said, "because all we really have on him so far is the van. We need to figure out if he's got access to insulin or if maybe one of these other guys do."

"Don't forget the myrrh oil," Patty said. "Now that we have only four good suspects, maybe I could take their photos around to the health food places. I can pull the pictures from the DMV."

"Good idea," Vicky said. "But we need to keep it low profile. Especially since we're investigating one of our own."

"How can you even call him that?" Boggs protested. "Jeez."

"If he's one of the mayor's pets, we've got to be careful. That's all I'm saying," Vicky added. "But I'm going to let Captain Billings in on what we've come up with so far."

"Are you sure he's okay?" Johnnie asked. She was typing again. "I'm going to see if he's also a member of The Fellowship." A few moments later she looked up from her laptop. "Doesn't look like it."

"I'm positive the captain is okay," Vicky said. "And his sister is gay, so he's very open and accepting." She pulled out her phone and went over to the other side of the room to make her call. She returned to her spot on the couch five minutes later. "Captain Billings was furious about the whole Peter thing. He said he's wondered about *The Fellowship* for quite a while. There was a guy who the mayor wanted on the police force, as a lieutenant, no less. Captain Billings said this guy hadn't even gone through the police academy, but the mayor kept pushing. Thankfully, there's a city statute that requires all police officers to be graduates of an academy." Vicky took a long drink of beer. "He wants us to keep digging on Peter, but keep everything very low profile. He believes the mayor has long arms."

"Long arms?" Patty asked.

"Meaning he's got people on the police force," Vicky said.

"And probably in the fire department and every other city agency," Boggs added. "And we know he has Peter."

"I'm glad Captain Billings is involved now," Toni said. "He definitely had our back last year when we were dealing with that whole Dexter thing." Toni tapped her fingers on the rim of her beer bottle.

"What?" Vicky asked. "Did you think of something?"

"Cathy told us our guy was using a list, or maybe two lists, right?" Toni said slowly. "And maybe it is like we thought, the Fairfield Human Rights Campaign. Either way, I think that means he's already picked out his victims. Maybe we can find the link here."

"Well, I was able to find out the name of the doctor and dentist of Maggie and John," Patty said. "Completely different. Not even in the same medical building, so I guess that angle's out." She shrugged.

"Crap," Vicky said. "That would have been perfect. I was really liking the crazy doctor idea." She held an imaginary microphone in front of her face. "Local dentist drills his victims with rocks." She smiled. "Obviously the stress of this case is getting to me."

Johnnie laughed. "Well, the media isn't helping much," she said. "Did you see that idiot on Channel Four last night? She worked herself into a frenzy describing the murder of the dad guy. What's his name again?"

"Joshua Andrew," Patty said.

"At least we've been able to keep the connection out of the media," Vicky said. "Captain Billings did a really good job at that press conference about Mr. Andrew. And of course no one knows about the prostitutes or Amy Judge."

"What about the noisy neighbor?" Boggs asked. "Will she talk to the press? She obviously saw Amy duct taped to a chair."

Vicky grinned. "I kind of told her that Amy's girlfriend was a bit nuts. I acted like I was confiding in her and told her not to spread that information around. If I read her correctly, she will have told the entire neighborhood that story by now. Anyway, Captain Billings didn't release anything about the victims being duct taped or stoned."

"Very clever about the neighbor," Toni said. "Aside from the panic this would cause in the community, I think that a lot of press would add to this guy's delusions."

"How so?" Patty asked.

"He might start thinking that he's invincible or that the news reporters were actually congratulating him," Toni replied. "When you're *really* delusional, you only hear what you want to hear and twist everything else. For example, if someone flipped this guy off, he'd never think it was because of his own conduct. He'd probably think that the guy was jealous of his greatness.

And it just gets more and more out of control."

"How the hell did you work with these crazy people?" Johnnie asked. "It makes my head spin. I'll stick to regular crime, thank you very much."

"But, Johnnie, *you* think like criminals," Toni said. "You have to if you want to figure out either their next step or maybe where they're hiding. So you *do* work with crazy people."

"And you hang out with us," Vicky added. "Let's see what we need to do." She flipped through her notepad. "Patty and I will show some photos at the health food stores and see if we get any hits. Plus, we'll keep digging into all these guys. And, Toni, if you'll check out old court documents to see if we can find a diagnosis for Mevin?" She jotted down a couple lines and put the tip of her pen in her mouth. "Am I missing anything?"

Patty had her own notepad. "You said Claire would call you if Amy woke up, right?"

"Yeah. And she'll be notified if it happens when she's gone from the hospital."

"Then it sounds like we've done all we can do right now," Patty said as she closed both her laptop and her notepad.

"Let's talk about something happy for a few minutes," Toni said. "I need to know what you guys are bringing for Thanksgiving."

"Claire and I are bringing apple pie, wine and some weird bread," Vicky said.

Toni had grabbed a pad of paper and a pen from the bar. "What the hell is weird bread?"

"I have no idea but it's something that Claire is making."

Toni grinned as she wrote down the items. She looked at Patty.

"I'm going to bring a corn casserole," Patty said. "It's an old family recipe. And some kind of dessert. Maybe brownies."

"Sounds perfect. What about you?" She looked at Johnnie.

"I'm thinking that a case of beer and a couple cases of soda would be good for me," Johnnie said.

"Old family recipe?" Boggs asked.

"Absolutely," Johnnie said. "My family drinks a lot."

Toni laughed. "Works for me. Dinner will be at about two o'clock, but feel free to come over at noon. Football will be on every television, but if you come early you're also agreeing to work."

"Sounds fair to me," Vicky said.

The conversation turned to previous Thanksgiving dinners and they all tried to top each other for having the worst family gathering.

"It was a perfect day," Vicky began. "That chilly kind of day with beautiful blue skies and leaves falling." She was obviously getting into a storytelling mode. She grinned. "We were gathered at my parents' house, but my sister was in charge of roasting the turkey. She and her husband were stoned out of their minds, although I doubt my folks realized it at the time. My sister forgot to take the giblets and stuff out of the turkey and somehow the paper bag that they come in caught on fire. That damn turkey stayed in the oven forever, but when it came out it was blackish on the outside and still raw on the inside, despite the burnt bag. I'm thinking it wasn't thawed. The mashed potatoes were chunky, just about as bad as the gravy. My mom was drunk before the turkey even went in the oven. For dessert we had frozen apple pie. My mom just let it thaw, didn't cook it."

"Holy crap," Toni said, still laughing. "You totally win."

They told a few more stories, but none came close to Vicky's family fiasco. It was a nice way to try to forget the task at hand—catching a serial killer who was targeting gays.

# Chapter 14

Toni had been sitting at her desk for only about fifteen minutes on Wednesday morning when Charlie called.

"Hi, Toni," he began. "I've been keeping a close eye on Frank Watson and I'm thinking he's our guy."

"What makes you think so?"

"Well, I can't really say," he said. "But he said a few things in group therapy that really pissed me off. He has inappropriate thoughts, that's all I can tell you. Have there been any more incidents?"

Toni realized she needed to tread carefully. "You'd have to check with Detective Carter about that," she said. "They only come across my desk after they've been arrested."

Charlie sighed. "Yeah, I guess you're right. Oh, well."

Is he really that disgusted with Vicky just because she's gay, she wondered. *God, that really pisses me off.* She tried to shake the feeling and concentrate on what he was saying.

"Hey, why don't I tail the guy? Then I could call it in when I see him go up to a house."

"I don't know, Charlie." She appreciated his enthusiasm about trying to catch the imaginary Peeping Tom, but his treatment of Vicky and anyone he perceived to be gay was upsetting, to say the least. He was getting on her nerves.

"If I followed the son of a bitch," he continued, "I could keep him from hurting some woman."

"That's probably true," she said, trying to think of an excuse. She didn't want him harassing an innocent guy. "But there might be some problems if I tried to put you on the stand. You're also his therapist, remember?" She was congratulating herself for thinking of that.

"Oh, you're right. Maybe if I just try to keep close tabs on him? You know, making notes about his schedule and maybe I'll do a sign-out sheet for the van," he said.

Now that's something we could actually use, Toni thought. If Mevin's the one, then having a record of who had the van, or didn't have the van would help. "That's a fantastic idea, Charlie."

"I'm going to do that now," he said. "Let me know what I can do. And I'm more than willing to sit on a surveillance team. Unofficially, of course." He paused for a moment. "And I hope you and Jake can make the trivia night fundraiser this weekend. We're expecting a big crowd."

"Oh, gosh, Charlie. We won't be able to make it." She tried to sound somewhat sincere. If Charlie wasn't such a bigoted ass, a trivia night fundraiser was something she and Boggs would love to do. "Jake has to go out of town," she added. "And I don't like to go places without him." She snickered to herself.

"I completely understand," Charlie said. "I'll let you know when we have another one and maybe you can make it then. Who knows," he added, "you might be married by then."

"A girl can only hope," Toni replied, suppressing a giggle. She couldn't wait to tell this to Boggs. She thanked Charlie, but felt a bit unsettled after hanging up the phone. She knew he was trying to help catch a Peeping Tom and that was admirable. But she also knew that he wouldn't have given her the time of day if he thought she was a lesbian. It was only her lie about her relationship with Jake that enabled her to get the names of his clients. She called Vicky to update her on Charlie's plan.

"That might help," Vicky said. "Although I seriously doubt he'd actually sign out the van to go and kill someone, we might be able to eliminate him. For example, if we knew that someone else had that van Monday night, we'd know it wasn't him."

"That's what I was thinking," Toni said. "I hate lying to him about both the Peeping Tom and Jake, but we could use the information."

"Agreed," Vicky said. "I'll keep you posted on my end." She hung up, as usual, without saying anything else.

Toni began her own investigation by looking up all the court documents pertaining to Mevin Murran. Most of the time, documents relating to someone's mental health were filed under seal and the general public was not allowed to see them. Fortunately, she was not the general public and she was able to view everything on her computer.

After almost thirty minutes, she hit pay dirt. Mevin's defense counsel had filed a sentencing memorandum with the court a year ago when he was convicted of the assault. It requested leniency based on his childhood and mental health issues. She printed the document and tucked it in her briefcase to review later. She was due in court in less than fifteen minutes for a preliminary hearing and the rest of her day was equally as busy.

The man left his job around four o'clock on Wednesday afternoon with a smile on his face. He felt like he was walking on air. God had been sending him messages through music all day. On his way to work he heard the song "Still the One." Later in the morning he heard "Killing Me Softly" in the elevator and then "The Sound of Silence." He spent his lunch hour sitting outside in the cold drizzle praying for guidance. He was puzzled at first until he realized that these messages were about his personal list of people to cast out, not God's list. He immediately understood the messages and couldn't help but grin. It took all the restraint he could muster to finish out most of his workday.

He drove home, gave his mother a kiss on her cheek and headed straight to his sanctuary. He was almost too excited to concentrate on his task. He twisted his ring as he sat at his desk. He knew he needed to do some research, but he also knew that God would protect him. It only took about an hour for him to make his decision with two possible backup targets. He went into his bedroom to change his clothing just a few minutes before his mother called him down for dinner. He quickly found his 9mm handgun in the top of his closet and grabbed a box of ammunition next to it. After loading the weapon, he put the ammunition back in the closet. He tucked the gun behind his back in the waistband of his jeans and pulled his sweatshirt over the bulge. He located the silencer for this gun in his top drawer and slid it in his back pocket before going downstairs to eat his mother's meatloaf, mashed potatoes and lima beans.

After finishing his dinner, he made an excuse to his mother and left. He had to sit in his van for several minutes just to calm himself. He prayed for another five minutes before driving to his first, and hopefully only, destination.

He knew that the deviant lived in a four-family flat. He prayed that she lived alone, but if need be, he'd kill whoever was there with her. This was his list, after all. He picked her as his first because she flaunted herself as a sinner to the entire community. She was a firefighter and had saved a young girl earlier this year. She was interviewed on the local news and she actually told the reporter that her partner was also a firefighter. He almost vomited when the camera panned over to another woman. He couldn't believe that the fire chief allowed such things and that the news would blatantly report it. *Maybe they reported it so that I could do my work for God.* That realization made him smile.

He got out of his van and pulled on an old sweatshirt jacket, zipping it all the way up. He walked up to the front of the building with his gym bag in his hand. As like most of the four-family flats on the west side of town, there was a single door that led to the interior doors. Once inside he pulled out his gun and quickly screwed on the silencer. He slipped the weapon into his front waistband this time, before taking a quick look around. He twisted his ring before knocking on the door. He could hardly contain his excitement.

When the door opened, he recognized her immediately from the news report, and he felt his heart beat faster. He delivered his rehearsed line perfectly and stepped across the threshold. "This is a delicate investigation," he continued. "Several women have complained about harassment by the Deputy Fire Chief. Is it okay for me to talk to you here? Are you alone?"

"Yes," she said. "It's just me here right now. We can talk in the living room."

She turned away from him, and as she walked toward her living room, he pulled out his gun and shot her in the back of the head. He'd been inside for less than five seconds. The sound of the gunshot was a little louder than he remembered, but not too bad. Just a little louder than a firecracker. No one would think twice about it in this neighborhood. He looked at her lifeless body on the floor. There was no question that she was dead. He opened his gym bag and carefully put his gun in the bottom. He slipped on a pair of latex gloves and pulled out a Bible. He said a short prayer before placing it next to the body. After placing the myrrh oil on her neck, he was ready to leave. He was very disappointed that the gunshot ruined an opportunity to place the oil on her forehead, but he felt good about his mission. Once he'd closed the front door behind him, he pulled off the gloves and shoved them in his front pocket. As soon as he got to his car, he took off the jacket and quickly tied it up in a knot, casually throwing it in the passenger seat. He drove away feeling very satisfied and was humming the song "Still the One" quietly to himself. On the other side of town, he tossed the jacket in a Dumpster behind an Italian restaurant. He figured that whatever spatter was on the jacket would look similar to pasta and sauce. He was back home in less than an hour.

# Chapter 15

"Your cat just stole a carrot," Toni yelled from the kitchen. She followed Little Tuffy into the living room and saw the carrot in the middle of the room. Boggs was sitting on the couch watching a college football game. Toni stopped and pointed to the chewed orange stick on the rug and repeated her statement.

Boggs almost spit out her beer, laughing. "My cat? Since when did he become *my* cat?"

"Since always," Toni replied. She picked up the carrot. "I turned my back for one minute and he took it right off the cutting board."

A flash of gray fur went past both of them. Little Tuffy had another carrot stick in his mouth. He had picked up speed as he flew across the rug, but as he attempted to negotiate a turn on the hardwood floor, he ended up skidding into the sliding glass door. He dropped the carrot but kept on going. Toni laughed so hard it took her a couple minutes to realize that he was on the kitchen counter once again. By the time she got back to the kitchen Little

Tuffy had yet another carrot stick and was heading up the stairs.

"I guess I have to guard all vegetables," she said, still laughing.

Boggs had brought the stolen carrots back in the kitchen, including the one he left on the steps. "First asparagus and now carrots. He's such a strange cat," she said. "I think he comes from your side of the family."

"I'm going to take that as a compliment." Toni finished cleaning the carrots for their lunches and put them in the refrigerator. She sat at the kitchen island and took out her list of things to do for Thanksgiving. Boggs sat next to her as they planned their first holiday gathering. When the doorbell rang, they both looked at the monitor, somewhat puzzled.

"I wonder what Vicky wants," Boggs said as she headed toward the front door. "And why she didn't call first. That's not like her."

Vicky came in the kitchen and dropped an overnight bag on the floor. Toni knew it was the one she always kept in her car in case she had an unexpected hot date. She sat next to Toni. "I need a beer," she said quietly.

Boggs grabbed one from the refrigerator and opened it for her. "What happened?"

Vicky took several gulps before answering. "Linda Dahl is dead."

"Firefighter Linda?" Boggs asked.

Vicky nodded slowly.

"Was there a fire?" Toni asked. She'd never met Linda, but had heard both Boggs and Vicky talk about her. She and Vicky had gone to high school together.

Vicky said nothing and downed the rest of her beer. She held the empty bottle up in the air. "I'm spending the night in your guest room, so keep them coming, Boggs. I left a message for Claire, so she might call here."

"What happened?" Toni asked again. She grabbed a handful of tissues from a box on the counter and set them next to Vicky.

"It looks like our maniac has changed his method," she began.

"She was shot in the back of the head, inside her apartment. The Bible was there." She took another drink. "We didn't know for sure it was the same guy until the M.E. found myrrh oil on her neck. I had him check."

"On her neck?" Toni was confused.

"There wasn't a forehead left," Vicky said, her face pale. She took several more gulps of her beer. "Her partner found her this morning. She's also a firefighter."

"Oh, my, God," Toni whispered. She put her arm around Vicky's shoulders and squeezed. "I'm so sorry, honey. Is there something I can do for you?"

Vicky shook her head. Tears ran down her cheek. She dried them with the sleeve of her blazer. "I need to catch this bastard," she hissed.

"You will, Vic," Boggs said.

The doorbell rang again. "That's probably Patty and Johnnie," Vicky said. "I hope you don't mind."

"Of course we don't mind, sweetie." Toni let them in and Boggs got drinks for everyone. The group quietly headed downstairs to the basement. Toni could feel the sadness and desperation in the air. Johnnie sat in her usual spot at the end of the bar and opened her laptop. Patty sat next to her with her own laptop.

Patty broke the silence. "This doesn't make any sense to me," she said. "Why would he shoot Linda? Why not do the same thing with the stun gun?"

"Maybe he didn't have enough time," Johnnie said. "Maybe someone came around and he panicked or something. Did you guys do a canvass of the area?"

"Yeah, we did," Vicky said. She was on her third beer and had apparently gone from distraught over the death of her friend to anger. "No one heard or saw a God damned thing. What's wrong with people? Don't they look out for their neighbors?"

"We did talk to an older lady who lives in the building," Patty said. "She lives upstairs on the other side. She didn't see anything out of the ordinary, but she thought she heard a firecracker that afternoon."

"So the guy must have used a silencer," Johnnie said. "And if it sounded like a firecracker, it was probably a nine millimeter or a thirty-eight."

"It was a nine millimeter," Vicky confirmed. "We found the slug in the wall."

"I'm assuming it was in no condition to do any decent ballistic testing," Johnnie said.

"No, it wasn't."

"What was the time of death according to the M.E.?" Boggs asked.

"Between two and six yesterday afternoon," Vicky replied.

"I guess that's a time when a lot of folks aren't home from work yet," Toni said. "Maybe that's why no one saw anything."

Patty thumbed through their list from the Fairfield Human Rights Campaign. "She's on the list here. Linda Dahl is right here. What is her partner's name?"

Vicky's eyes began to tear up. "Her name is Debbie Harper," she said quietly.

"She's on here too." Patty tossed the papers on the bar. "This is crazy."

"At least it was quick," Boggs said.

Vicky glared at her.

"I mean, well, you said she was shot in the back of the head. That means she didn't see it coming and it was over in a flash." Boggs looked at the floor. "No disrespect or anything, but at least she wasn't tortured." She kept her eyes lowered. "I guess that doesn't sound right."

Toni rubbed her back. "I understand what you're saying, hon. And I agree. At least that's something."

Vicky took a deep breath. "You're right, Boggs. I'm sorry. This is beginning to be too much. We've got to figure this bastard out. Maybe Johnnie's right and he got spooked and that's why he used a gun."

"I don't think so," Toni said quietly. Everyone looked at her. "I think this is different. Maybe it's a second list like Cathy said."

"Why the hell would he do that?" Patty asked.

"No clue," Toni said. "But it makes sense to him. Not to us, but to him. I'm sure of that."

"Maybe he's one of those multiple kind of people," Johnnie said. "And one of them uses a stun gun and the other uses a real gun." Her sarcasm wasn't hard to mistake.

"Very funny," Toni replied, "but you might have something there. Not two different personalities, but two separate things. Same result, but I'm thinking he sees this as different."

"I'm not sure I understand," Vicky said. "But if someone will get me another beer, I might be able to figure it out." Her frustration and anger were apparent.

Johnnie was closest, so she pulled out a bottle of beer from the little refrigerator, popped off the cap and handed it to Patty. Patty leaned back and handed it to Vicky, who rolled her eyes. "Gee, don't put yourself out or anything, Johnnie." She took a long drink and nodded to Toni. "Go ahead."

"Okay, I'm going to go on the assumption that Cathy was correct when she saw two lists. She's been dead-on in the past."

"Bad choice of words, babe." Boggs grinned.

"Sorry. Anyway, I think that he's got two missions or whatever," Toni continued. "One is far more structured, or at least it feels that way. He zaps the person first, then goes to the trouble of duct taping them to a chair. It's as though he needs them as an audience or something. Otherwise, why not just kill them immediately? Like he did with Linda."

"That makes sense to me," Boggs said. "So maybe this guy performs some kind of ritual that he wants the victim to see."

"Exactly," Toni said. "I'm thinking he does all that before he administers the insulin. Then he ends it with the rock or stone."

"That means if Amy wakes up, she'd be able to tell us," Vicky said. "If that's the pattern, then she definitely saw the guy and heard everything. The neighbor interrupted him just as he was starting to inject the medicine."

"We've got to figure out the connection between these people," Toni said.

"You don't think it's just people on the list?" Patty asked.

"You think there's something else?"

"I do," Toni said, "but I'm not sure what it is. It's obvious to him, but not to us. At least not yet."

"What about the two prostitutes?" Johnnie said. "How do they fit it? They aren't on the list."

"Shit, that's right," Toni said. "But wait, maybe that will help us anyway. What if our killer started out with these two women, then graduated to the list? It might be easier to find the connection the two of them share. Can we find out more about them?"

Vicky sat up straighter now, and although she was definitely a bit impaired, she was able to focus a little more. "Hey, Johnnie. How about getting me a Coke? And Patty, let's see if we can interview more people who knew either of these two women. The prostitutes, I mean. I think Toni might be on to something here. What were their names again?"

Patty flipped through her notebook while Johnnie retrieved a Coke from the refrigerator. This time Johnnie actually handed the can to Vicky.

"I've got it right here," Patty said. "Okay, the first one was Catherine Geneis and she's the one who died over a month ago of a drug overdose. The second one was Irene Levitch and we haven't been able to find her yet."

"How sure are we that she died of a drug overdose?" Toni asked. "Since she was a prostitute, how close did the M.E. look?"

"Good point," Vicky said. "Although I'm not sure there's much we can do about that now. Are you thinking that our maniac might have returned to finish the job?"

"Just a thought," Toni replied. "I figured we needed to keep an open mind."

"Very true. Okay," Vicky said after a slug of Coke. "Patty, check and see if you can get their Social Security numbers or something from the police reports. Or maybe from arrest records, because I'm pretty sure they were both picked up more than once, although I doubt they did any state time."

It only took about five minutes for Patty to get the information. "Can you look them up?" Vicky asked Johnnie. "And do some fancy cross-checking to see if you can locate their parents or siblings or something?"

"I'll do my best," Johnnie said as she lit a cigarette. "I'm not sure about the siblings on short notice, but I can get the names and addresses for the parents." She hit several keys. After several minutes, she grinned. "I've got the first one. Are you ready?" she asked Patty.

"Go."

"Catherine Geneis's father was Pierre Geneis. He died in 1995. Her mother's name is Antoinette Bridges. She apparently remarried in 1998 and she lives here in Fairfield."

"Are they French?" Boggs asked. "Was Catherine a French citizen or a United States citizen? Not that it matters, but it might be relevant."

"Her parents were from France, but she was born here," Johnnie replied. She read off the address of Catherine's mother. "It doesn't look like she had any brothers or sisters."

"Well, at least we have an address for the mother," Vicky said. "Thank you. What about the second woman, Irene? The one we can't seem to find."

While Johnnie was looking up the information, Vicky leaned over to Toni. "Could I trouble you for some coffee? I think I'd like to kill this buzz from the beer, and the Coke just isn't cutting it."

"Absolutely," Toni said. "I'm making a pot of coffee," she announced to the gang. "And bringing down some cookies to munch on. Who wants some?"

Whether it was the chill of the night or the fact that they all thought they'd be up for several more hours, everyone wanted coffee. Toni went upstairs and started a full pot. While it was brewing, she gathered Oreos and some chocolate chip cookies from the cupboard. She also grabbed a box of Girl Scout Thin Mints that she had put in the freezer. She figured they would thaw pretty quickly. Once the coffee had finished, she poured the entire pot into a large carafe and set it on a tray along with the cookies and small paper plates. She grabbed five mugs from the cabinet and a few spoons. There was half-and-half in the refrigerator downstairs, as well as sugar and liquor if anyone wanted their coffee spiked. She carried the loaded tray downstairs and set it on the table.

"Now I know why they call this a coffee table," Toni said. "This is strictly a self-serve place, so help yourselves. I'll pour the first cup, but you have to add your own fixin's."

"Did you actually say fixin's?" Vicky asked.

"Yes, I did," Toni said with a grin. "And these here vittles are fancy store-bought cookies."

Vicky rolled her eyes while stuffing two Oreos in her mouth at the same time.

Boggs had already gotten the things they needed from the bar and for the next couple of minutes everyone busied themselves making their coffee and grabbing cookies.

"Thanks, Toni," Vicky said in between bites of still frozen Thin Mints. After taking several sips of coffee, she continued, "tomorrow, Patty and I will track down the parents."

"Hey, did you guys ask around the health food stores?" Toni asked.

"Sure did," Patty said after finishing the rest of her Oreo. "One guy knew Peter, but only because he'd questioned him about a burglary last spring. No one else knew any of the guys."

"What pictures did you show?" Boggs asked.

"We used the photos from their driver's license," Vicky said. "We showed them Peter, Joe the weird neighbor, Mevin and David Davidson."

"But I found a conflict for David Davidson this morning," Patty said. "So I think he's off our list."

"What was it?" Johnnie asked.

"He was at a wedding in Chicago when Maggie was killed. I double-checked."

"Well, he wasn't high on our list anyway," Vicky said.

"I guess there's a good possibility that our guy ordered the

127

myrrh oil from the Internet," Boggs said. "That's how I do most of my shopping."

"I think you're probably right," Vicky said. "I figured it was a long shot, but worth a try. I even asked the store managers if they could track who bought the oil, but they don't have that capability. They're pretty small stores."

"Okay," Johnnie said as she hit a few more keys, "I've got the info on Irene. Both parents are dead, killed in a car accident. Her dad was a rabbi. The only address listed for her in any of my databases is her parents'. It looks like she always used that as an address, even after they died. Hey, wait a minute." She keyed in several more things. "I thought that address sounded familiar."

"Someone else's? Maybe one of our suspects?" Patty asked.

"No such luck," Johnnie said. "The parents lived on Concord Street, across from the mall."

"Oh, where those new restaurants are?" Toni asked.

"Yup. Irene was using the address even after all those houses were torn down for the new construction." Johnnie shook her head. "There is nothing recent on her. This girl is either dead or has disappeared."

"I agree," Patty said looking at her own screen. "Over the past year or so, she was picked up about once every few weeks. Usually for soliciting or shoplifting, but since the assault where our guy bonked her on the head, she's been clean. That doesn't make sense to me."

"So either she decided to make a new life for herself because of the trauma," Toni said, "or she's dead. Maybe he found her."

"Bastard," Vicky muttered.

"So how are these girls connected?" Boggs asked. "Is there something they share besides working the streets?"

"They are four years apart in age," Patty said, looking at her notes. "I doubt they knew each other in school."

"And Irene was Jewish," Johnnie said. "I doubt that Catherine was, so church is probably out, although we should double-check on that."

"Can we find out about what they did in high school?"

Boggs asked. "Maybe they both were into dance, or theatre or something."

"I'll do that tomorrow," Patty said. "It's worth a shot."

"What about the funerals?" Johnnie asked.

"Debbie will let me know," Vicky said.

"Okay," Johnnie said. "But I was wondering about the funerals of the other victims."

Vicky refilled her mug of coffee. Toni noticed her eyes were filling up with tears at the mention of Linda's funeral, but she wiped her eyes with her sleeve. She cleared her throat before responding. "The other funerals, right. Well, we all went to Maggie's, but none of us were thinking serial killer at that time. But, I went to the second one and Patty went to the third. We took photos of the crowd, but none of our suspects were there and no one stands out at all."

Johnnie nodded. "I was just wondering. I noticed that there weren't any protests or anything, so I'm thinking that the crazy Web site people aren't involved."

"I'm still thinking that there is some connection between the two women," Toni said again. "I can't shake that feeling. Maybe you'll find something at the schools, Patty." She refilled her own mug of coffee. "Oh, I got a sentencing memo from a year ago on Mevin," she added.

Boggs was chewing on a now thawed Thin Mint. "I love these damn things. So, what did it say?"

"There wasn't a lot of detail," Toni said after finishing a chocolate chip cookie. "But it's pretty interesting. It said that he's an only child, raised in a strict fundamentalist home."

"That will mess you up," Vicky said.

"No kidding. He had lots of behavior problems in both grade school and junior high school and was diagnosed as oppositional."

"What does that mean?" Patty asked.

"Pretty much that he won't do what adults tell him to do," Toni said. "Not a real serious thing as far as we're concerned. His dad abandoned the family when he was twelve, but the memo didn't say why. And at the time of his assault conviction, it said he was suffering from bipolar disorder."

"That's the up and down one, right?" Patty asked.

Toni smiled. "That's an excellent description, yes. It used to be called manic-depressive disorder," she continued. "It means that you have episodes of both. Some folks try to self-medicate with alcohol or drugs. It can be mild or very severe. Some even have psychotic episodes."

"That fits," Vicky said. "He got the DWIs about the same time. But what about being delusional? Would that fit?"

"Hard to say," Toni said, "but it does make me wonder. We now know that he's had mental health issues in the past along with a crappy childhood. If some other event happened around the same time, maybe that pushed him over the edge. But here's the kicker. It said he's a diabetic. I say he is a good contender."

"Holy crap," Johnnie said. "I agree."

"Me, too," Boggs added. "But I keep thinking about this guy being intelligent. This maniac, as Vic likes to call him, is smart. And he knows what he's doing. He doesn't leave any evidence."

"I think Mevin's smart enough," Vicky said. "He made it through nursing school. And he's obviously got access to insulin, whether it be his own or working at the hospital."

"And there's something about him," Toni added. "I think he would be able to talk his way into a lot of people's houses."

"Didn't you say that Charlie was going to do a sign-out sheet for the van?" Vicky asked.

"Yes. He calls me at least once a day, sometimes more, leaving messages. He's positive that this one guy is responsible for the Peeping Tom thing. He's getting on my nerves."

"How come?" Patty asked.

"Well, I appreciate that he's trying to help, don't get me wrong," Toni said. "But just knowing that he wouldn't give me the time of day if he knew I was a lesbian, that pisses me off."

"You're a lesbian?" Boggs asked, acting horrified. "If I'd have known that, I'd never have suggested we live together."

"Guess you're stuck now," Toni said with a smile on her

face.

"Ick," Johnnie added. "I hope you don't rub off on the rest of us."

Toni rolled her eyes at all of them. "Anyway, I'll call Charlie tomorrow and ask him to fax me the sign-out sheet. Not that I think Mevin would sign out the van to go and kill someone, but maybe it will give us more information."

"True," Vicky said.

"And let's ask Claire if she knows Mevin, or ever worked with him," Boggs said. "Just because he works at Christian Hospital now doesn't mean he didn't work at other hospitals when he was a nurse."

"Good idea," Vicky said as she pulled out her phone. "And I'll check and see how Amy is doing."

While Vicky was on the phone, the others talked about other possible connections between the first two women. They looked at everything from hair and eye color to build and probable shoe size. Nothing made any sense.

"Do you want the bad news or the bad news?" Vicky said as she rejoined them.

"Crap," Johnnie said as she lit a cigarette.

"Amy Judge died a couple of minutes ago. Claire was just getting ready to call. She never regained consciousness."

"Oh, I'm so sorry," Toni said quietly. "At least she didn't suffer. Well, you know what I mean. Jeez, that didn't come out right."

"I know what you're saying." Boggs squeezed her shoulder.

"What's the other bad news?" Johnnie asked.

"Claire never heard of our guy, but she is going to ask around. Discreetly, of course."

"I've been thinking about what Boggs said," Johnnie said. "And I think she might be right about our guy being smart. But not just book smart, forensic smart."

"Exactly," Boggs said. "He hasn't left any evidence. He's obviously wearing gloves and there are no prints on the stones or the Bibles. That's why I'm leaning toward Peter. Plus, I think he's a total asshole."

"I'm leaning in that direction," Vicky said. "Even though Mevin has a lot of red flags. That could explain how he gets inside these apartments. Flash a badge."

"Son of a bitch," Boggs growled. "I knew I never liked the guy."

"Doesn't mean it's him," Vicky warned. "We've got to get proof. So don't *accidentally* shoot the bastard, okay?"

"Hey!" Toni sat up straight, almost spilling her mug of coffee. "Call Claire back. Has she notified anyone that Amy died? Can you tell her not to?"

Vicky was already dialing. "Dammit. Why didn't I think of that? Patty, call Captain Billings and tell him what we're going to do."

Vicky was excited now, and she hopped up and began pacing. She began talking quickly to Claire, giving her instructions.

Patty looked confused at first, but after hearing Vicky explain things to Claire, she dialed her own phone and explained their plan to Captain Billings.

"This just might work," Johnnie said. "If he thinks that Amy has regained consciousness, he'll have to make a move to silence her. He's got to be worried."

"A normal person would be worried," Toni said. "But not necessarily him. He might think that if she identifies him, it is because God wants everyone to know about him. But I think it's worth a shot. Hard to say. He might think that it's not time, and in that scenario he'd kill her."

"I am so tired of these crazy people," Johnnie said. "But I guess it is job security."

Both Vicky and Patty finished their phone calls about the same time.

"Claire was still in the room with Amy when I called her back," Vicky said. "She talked to her supervisor and they aren't releasing her *condition*. At least not for the next twelve hours."

"How did you swing that?" Boggs asked.

"Her supervisor's dad is a cop, so she understood what was going on. Let me call Captain Billings and give him the update."

"How are we going to get the information out there?" Patty asked. "Our killer needs to know what's going on. Boggs could mention it to Peter, but what about our other suspects?"

"What about a press conference?" Johnnie suggested. "Maybe Captain Billings could give a statement about crime in general and mention that a recent victim of a home invasion is recovering and an arrest is imminent. That should make the news."

"Good idea," Vicky said. "I'll see what he thinks."

"Speaking of the press," Boggs said. "Guess who will be featured in tomorrow's paper?"

"Not featured," Toni said. "A small mention is more like it."

"What's the scoop?" Johnnie asked. "Did you win an award or something?"

"Far from it," Toni said. "Our office hires third-year law students every year and I've been helping supervise a group of them this fall. It's just a small article about how the prosecutor's office contributes to public interest groups. I only talked to the reporter for about five minutes. I doubt they'll even mention my name. I think they talked to Anne Mulhoney for quite a while. She is *the* prosecutor."

"Still, I think it's pretty cool," Boggs said. "My girl is famous."

Vicky closed her phone and finished the last of her coffee. "Captain Billings is going for the press conference idea. He's doing it in the morning. He's also going to call Claire's supervisor and set things up. I think he wants to put a dummy or something in the bed and make it obvious that it is supposed to be Amy's room. I don't know if he can swing it, but it's worth a shot. Maybe this will be the break we need."

"If it turns out to be Mevin, he'd know what was up. He was a nurse, you know," Patty said.

"True," Vicky said. "But if he's nosing around, that would at least give us something a little more definitive. We could bring him in for questioning and maybe get a warrant to search his place." She looked at Toni. "So you're going to be a media star, huh? Will you still associate with us peons?"

"Sure," Toni said. "I'll remember all of you. I'll be sitting in my yacht and say to Boggs, 'do you remember those women we used to hang around with?' Yeah, I'll definitely remember you."

"Very funny." Vicky stood. "I think I'm okay to head home. No sense in spending the night here. I'm sober and Claire is on her way over to my place. Can't disappoint the doc."

"Yeah, we should be heading out, too," Johnnie said.

Toni, Boggs and Vicky all looked at Johnnie with their eyebrows raised.

Johnnie blushed and Patty turned away, busying herself with her laptop. "Yes, it's true," Johnnie continued. "Patty and I are dating in case you all are too stupid to realize that." She grinned. "At least until she gets tired of me."

It was Patty's turn to blush and her face was as red as a beet when she turned to face the group. She was also grinning. Johnnie leaned over and kissed her on the cheek. "I guess I outed us," she said.

"It's not like we didn't know," Vicky said. "As long as you two aren't as mushy as these guys," she added, pointing to Toni and Boggs, "then we're good."

They headed upstairs, agreeing to meet again tomorrow night. Boggs carried the tray with the carafe and mugs. There were no cookies left. Not even any crumbs. After Boggs set the alarm, she and Toni put the mugs in the dishwasher.

"Do you think this ruse will work?" Toni asked.

"I sure hope so. I think it's Peter and I think he'll make a move if he thinks Amy can identify him. Come on," she said, taking Toni's hand. "Let's go to bed." She winked.

"Are you tired?" Toni asked.

"Not at all."

The huge grin on Toni's face was all Boggs needed for a response.

# Chapter 16

Boggs was sitting at the kitchen island drinking a cup of coffee and reading the newspaper on Friday morning when Toni came down the stairs.

"There's actually an entire paragraph about you, babe," Boggs said.

"Are you kidding?" Toni poured coffee in her travel mug and sat next to Boggs. Mr. Rupert was sitting on the island. He pawed at the paper that was lying flat on the countertop.

"See? Even Mr. Rupert is impressed."

"Let me see that." Toni pulled the paper closer at which point Mr. Rupert promptly sat his large self in the middle. "Come on, boy. I want to read."

He plopped down and rolled over on his side, covering the majority of the paper.

Boggs laughed. "Well, it basically said that you are one of the supervisors for law students at Metro and that you used to be a psychotherapist. It said you were a member of the bar, duh, as well as the American Counseling Association and the Gay and Lesbian Alliance. That's about it. You were right, it was mostly about Anne."

"Well, she is the boss," Toni said. Mr. Rupert was still covering the paper. "I guess I'll look at it later. He's too cute to move." She glanced at her watch. "Want to ride to work together? I'll treat us to biscuits at Hardee's."

"That's a deal." Boggs refilled both of their cups. "Just let me grab my briefcase and gun and I'll be right with you."

They took Toni's VW Bug since it was better on gas than Boggs's SUV. Toni backed out into the alley and waited while the garage door slowly closed. "Hey, there's J or Joe. Mr. Weirdo." She waved to their neighbor who was putting trash in the Dumpster. "Might as well be friendly in case he's not the maniac," she said to Boggs.

He stood next to the Dumpster, looking at both of them for a moment, then turned and walked back to his house. It seemed obvious that he had seen them.

"Well, that was incredibly rude," Toni said as she drove past. "I saw him look right at us."

"If he were normal, he'd have grinned from ear to ear," Boggs said. "To have a pretty woman wave at him. Bet that's never happened in his entire life."

"Or maybe he's the maniac," Toni said quietly. She drove in silence for several minutes.

"We're okay, babe." Boggs reached over and rubbed her leg. "We've got the best security system ever made. And we're armed."

Toni shook her head. "I'm not."

"Maybe you should carry until this thing is over," Boggs said. "But until we get home tonight, I don't want you to be alone, okay?"

Toni tried to sound more confident than she felt. "I'll be fine, hon. He's never hit anywhere but the person's home. And since we're riding together, I won't be home alone."

Earlier that morning, he had finished his early morning prayer session and was eating breakfast at the kitchen table. His mother had made him fried eggs and bacon. He was drinking his second cup of coffee when he saw the article in the paper. He faithfully read this liberal Fairfield paper every day so that he would know his enemies. As he read the article, he could feel his face get hot and his jaw tighten.

"Are you okay, son? You don't look so good. Are your eggs okay?" His mother hovered over him.

He tried to calm himself. He didn't want to take his rage out on his mother. *Honor thy mother and father.* He repeated that three times before he responded. "Yes, Mother. I'm fine. And your eggs were wonderful as usual." He stood, kissed his mother's cheek and headed to his sanctuary. "I must get ready for work now."

Once inside his beloved room, he knelt in prayer, asking God for strength. After nearly twenty minutes he began to feel better. He understood now that the article was another message from God. Just to make sure, he ran several checks on his computer. There was no doubt, the newspaper was accurate in its description. He twisted his ring. Toni Barston was a deviant. *How did I miss that?* He'd talked to the woman, for Heaven's sake. He bowed his head in prayer again. After only five minutes, he smiled. There was no need to be angry any more. He'd just add her to his own personal list.

He decided to run some errands instead of going straight to work that morning. Who cared if he was late? His only *real* work was his mission for God. He'd only been in his car for a few minutes when he heard the news conference by Captain Billings. He pulled into a grocery store parking lot to listen. At first, he was frustrated, then he felt shame. He had disappointed God once again. He hung his head. She was supposed to be one of the ones God had chosen to cast out, and now she was going to be fine. *Should I go and kill her now?*

His answer came minutes later from the radio. A commercial was playing for a maid service. The message was loud and clear. LET US TAKE CARE OF YOUR MESS. YOU'RE IN GOOD HANDS.

He smiled and thanked God. He would move on with God's

list and his own list. Life was good.

Toni was sitting at her desk, checking her e-mail. "Oh, crap."

"Good to see you too, Toni," Sam Clark said from her doorway.

Toni jumped at the sound of his voice. "Oh, sorry, Sam."

"Read something you don't like?"

"Actually, I did. I see that you assigned Peter as my investigator for the McConnell case."

"I know, that's why I came down," Sam said. He was leaning against the doorframe with a Diet Coke in his hand.

"Sit down, Sam. Please." She motioned toward the only other chair in her small office.

Sam grinned and plopped down in the chair. After another gulp of his soda, he shrugged. "Sorry about that, but everyone else is swamped. Plus I figured you'd only need a couple witness interviews, and he's okay with that."

"I shouldn't complain," Toni said. "I'm grateful for the help. And you're right. Unless something unusual happens, that's all I'll need. I think the defendant is going to plead guilty anyway. I just wanted to make sure I knew what I could do if the plea blew up and I had to go to trial."

"I normally give Peter to Anne Mulhoney," Sam said. "He thinks it's because he's so good and that's why he gets to work for *the* prosecutor, but actually it's because he doesn't treat her like dirt." He grinned. "But the funny thing is that Anne told me when she has an important case that needs more than routine work, she only wants Boggs." He inched forward in his chair. "Has she found anything good yet?" he whispered.

Toni shook her head. "But not for lack of trying," she said quietly.

Sam leaned back and sighed. "Damn it. I might start looking myself."

"As soon as she knows *anything*, she'll fill you in."

"Still on the short list I assume?"

"Yes."

"Okay." He stood and drained the last of his Diet Coke, tossing it in the trashcan next to her desk. "Oops," he said, retrieving the can. "I keep forgetting we have a recycle bin now." He turned to leave. "Thanks for understanding about this, Toni. Hopefully soon it won't be an issue. Oh, and Betty wanted me to tell you that in addition to the rolls and casserole we're bringing, she is also baking a pumpkin pie."

"Perfect. This should be a great dinner." Toni jotted down the extra pie on her list from her briefcase.

"The sign-out sheet," she said to herself, after putting her own list away. She placed the call to Charlie, but Clara said he hadn't arrived yet. Toni really didn't want to talk to him anyway, so she took a chance and asked Clara for the list. "He said he would fax me a copy, so maybe you could handle that for him?" She hoped Clara would agree.

"I guess that would be okay," Clara responded tentatively.

Toni gave her the number and hung up relieved. Now I can just let his daily phone calls go to voice mail, she thought.

She retrieved the fax a few minutes later and looked at the scrawled signatures. It gave her absolutely no information. Another dead end. At least it was worth a shot, she told herself. Maybe now I don't have to deal with Charlie.

Toni looked at her calendar and sighed. The rest of her day was pretty full until almost four o'clock. She gathered the files she'd need for the morning. There were three detention hearings and two arraignments. Mostly routine stuff, she thought. She'd have enough time to wolf down a sandwich at about twelve thirty, then she had four plea hearings scheduled for the afternoon. She was still amazed at how the legal system worked. Sometimes it felt like a production line. First, the case would be called by the bailiff. In Judge Crayton's courtroom, the bailiff looked like he was eighty years old. He would mumble the name of the defendant, then clearly call out the case number as though that number was far more important than the actual person's name. Toni glanced at her watch. She needed to concentrate on her job instead of the absurdities of the system.

After the first detention hearing was over, Toni left the courtroom and headed to the one across the hall. There were a few people seated in the back, mostly law students she assumed, but the defense table was empty. She knew she had at least fifteen minutes before the judge would appear, but she sat at the prosecutor's table anyway. She pulled out the file for this hearing and stared at her notes. Her mind wasn't on the hearing. It was on the maniac that was stoning people to death. She knew there was something very obvious and simple that she was missing, but for the life of her, she couldn't think of what it was. Maggie was dead. She felt a wave of nausea overtake her and she closed her eyes. For a split second, she felt a sense of terror, maybe the same kind that Maggie felt. *What's happening to me?* She took a deep breath and tried to calm herself. The nausea faded and she opened her eyes. She was staring off into space, unaware of her surroundings, when she felt a hand touch her shoulder. She jumped.

"Sorry. Did I scare you?" The old bailiff smiled down at her.

"I guess I was in another world," she replied. "What can I do for you?"

"The judge wants to speak with you in chambers," he said.

She looked over at the defense table. It was still empty. "By myself?" she asked. It was unusual for a judge to ask for only one attorney. In fact, there was a rule that prohibited it. The bailiff shrugged and Toni followed him back to the judge's chambers. He left her standing outside the heavy oak door. She knocked lightly and waited. No response. She knocked a little harder this time and heard the judge beckon her inside.

She opened the door and stood in the doorway, unsure of what she should do and why she was called in here. "You asked to see me, Judge?"

Judge Mildred Crayton waved her inside. She was semi-retired and only recently had moved back to criminal law. She had salt-and-pepper hair that was cut short, but stylish. Her bright blue eyes shined behind rectangle wired-rimmed glasses. She was smiling. "Sit down, Toni. And close the door, please. We have a few minutes."

Toni did as instructed, sitting in one of the leather club chairs in front of the judge's massive desk. She sat at attention, if that was possible, and waited for the judge to speak.

"This isn't an *ex parte* discussion," Judge Crayton said. "In fact, this isn't about the Smithson case at all."

Toni relaxed just a bit. *I guess I'm not in trouble.* She waited for the judge to continue.

"I've been talking to Anne Mulhoney," the judge continued, "and I'm a little concerned."

*Oh, crap. Maybe I am in trouble if she's talking to my boss.* Toni tried to keep her composure. She was racking her brain, trying to think of what she could have done wrong. *But if I screwed up, why isn't Anne lecturing me instead of the judge?*

Judge Crayton must have seen the look on Toni's face. "No, dear. You aren't in trouble." She smiled again. "I know that Detective Carter is working on these murders."

Toni felt her entire body relax. She trusted Judge Crayton completely and knew that she was above reproach. If Anne Mulhoney trusted someone, then Toni surely could.

"Anne and I have been conferring with Captain Billings about all this," she continued. "Off the record, of course. We know that you have your own little task force."

"We just help Vicky come up with ideas," Toni said. "Nothing that would interfere with my job." She wasn't sure if what she was doing was allowed.

"Oh, goodness, dear. I'm not reprimanding you." Judge Crayton smiled and shook her head. "Quite the opposite. I happen to know that you have a certain knack for this kind of thing. Anyway, I know that one of your suspects is Peter Johnson."

Toni wasn't quite sure how to respond. She knew that Vicky was keeping Captain Billings apprised of their investigation and ideas, but she had no idea it had gone further than that. She blinked a couple times and nodded.

"Now this is completely between you, me and the fence post," she continued. "Well, for your group also." Her voice was quieter now. "I've had some issues with our mayor for some time now," she said. "Nothing that was concrete, mind you, but issues nonetheless. I smell a rat, that's all. And my senses are pretty good if I do say so myself. I know that the mayor has taken Peter under his wing, so I just wanted to caution you all to be careful."

"You think that the mayor could cause some trouble for us?"

"Yes, unfortunately I do." The judge said slowly. "I just wanted to make sure you all kept a wary eye about." She looked at her watch. "It's almost time for me to take the bench."

Toni stood. "Thank you, Judge. I'll pass along this information."

Judge Crayton nodded.

Toni headed to the door and just as she was about to open it, the judge spoke again.

"Who all is in your group, Toni?"

"Well, there's Vicky Carter of course, Detective Patty Green, Agent Johnnie Layton and Boggs. I mean Investigator Boggsworth."

"You make a fine team. Keep up the good work." The judge looked at the papers on her desk. "See you in the courtroom."

Toni made her way back to the prosecutor's table in the courtroom. The defense counsel was already sitting at his table with his client. She barely had time to look at her notes again before the bailiff called for everyone to rise. It was a good thing the hearing was pretty routine, because Toni could hardly concentrate. Her mind was on the conversation she'd had with the judge.

The rest of the day flew by, with Toni going from one courtroom to another. During the afternoon she had two students with her and spent every free moment answering their questions and explaining different areas of the law. By the time she sat at her own desk it was nearly four fifteen and she felt exhausted. There was a Post-it note stuck to the arm of her chair. It had a drawing of a stick person with a heart in his hand. She grinned and placed it in her drawer along with the dozens of other similar notes. *God, I love that woman.*

As if on cue, Boggs appeared at her door. "Hiya, gorgeous. How about calling it quits early and giving a girl a ride home?"

"Thanks for the note," Toni replied.

"Just reminding you that you've got my heart," Boggs said, grinning. "Can you leave now or do you have more work to do?"

"I've always got more work to do," Toni said, "but nothing that can't wait until Monday. Let me just check my e-mail to make sure nothing drastic happened while I was in court."

Boggs sat and stretched out her legs. "I don't know about you, but I'm sure glad it's Friday. This was an incredibly long week. The good news is that next week is short."

Toni finished checking her e-mails. "I know. I can't believe it's almost Thanksgiving. Are you going to be able to take off Wednesday?"

"I think so. Anne's case pled today, so there won't be a trial on Monday. Sam said there wouldn't be a problem." She winked at Toni. "That means we'll have all day together. How about we plan on staying in bed the entire day?"

Toni grinned. "I like the way you think. As long as the house is clean, the only thing we really need to do is roast the first turkey. Once we throw it in the oven, we can have the day to ourselves." She gathered her things and grabbed her briefcase. "Come on, sweetie. Let's go home."

Boggs looked at her watch. "If we hurry, we'll have almost an hour before the gang comes over."

Toni grabbed her arm as she went out the door. "What are you waiting for?"

The doorbell rang at ten minutes until six.

"Shit," Toni said, rolling over and glancing at the clock on the nightstand. "Is it six o'clock already?"

Boggs kissed the back of her neck. "Let's ignore them."

The bell rang again, this time in several short bursts.

Toni laughed. "You know how Vicky is. She'll probably climb up the side of the house and knock on our window if we don't

143

answer."

Boggs grumbled as Toni got out of bed and pulled on her sweats and a long-sleeved T-shirt. She pulled out a pair of sweats from the dresser and threw them at Boggs. The doorbell rang again.

Boggs walked across the bedroom, buck naked, and pushed a button the intercom. She had the sweats in her hand. "Yes?" She sounded very serious.

Toni giggled. "Now that's a look I could get used to. Wait till I tell Vicky you answered in your birthday suit."

Boggs seemed to realize how funny that was and started laughing. Vicky was talking loudly. "Open the damn door. I'm freezing my butt off out here." Boggs continued to laugh and started dancing around the room, swinging the sweatpants above her head.

"I hear you guys laughing. What's going on? Let me IN."

Toni went over to the intercom. "I'll buzz you in, Vic. Meet us in the kitchen." She pushed the red button that unlocked the front door.

"Are you going to put those on or strut around naked?"

Boggs was still laughing. "I don't know why I think this is so funny," she said. "Just the thought of Vicky standing out there while we're in here undressed and everything." She shook her head. "I must be slaphappy or something." She pulled on the sweatpants and dug in the dresser for a sweatshirt. She slipped on a pair of moccasins and looked at Toni. "You might consider putting on a hat or something," she said, grinning.

Toni's hand went immediately to her hair. "Does it look awful?"

"Well, it looks like, um, it looks like you just got out of bed. And it's pretty obvious that you weren't just sleeping."

Toni felt her face flush. "That noticeable, huh?"

Boggs nodded, then wrapped her arms around her. "And I love that."

Toni kissed her and for a moment she was tempted to pull her back into bed. Instead, she pulled away, grabbed a baseball

144

hat from the top of the dresser and put it on. "Better?"

"You look good enough to eat," Boggs replied with a sly grin.

They went downstairs with their arms wrapped around each other. Vicky was sitting at the kitchen island with a beer in her hand. She was petting Mr. Rupert, who was sitting on the stool next to her. When she saw Toni and Boggs, she rolled her eyes. "Gee, did I interrupt something?"

Toni felt her face get hot. "Um, no, not at all," she stammered.

"Yes, you sure as hell did," Boggs said. "But fortunately for you, we were at a stopping point." She grinned. "And I need food and beverage to regain my strength."

Toni rolled her eyes this time and got a beer for herself and Boggs. "Now that you mention it, I am kind of hungry."

"I told Patty it was her turn to bring food," Vicky said after several sips of her beer. "I hope she doesn't stop by Subs R Us. I'm sick of those. In fact if she brings those, I say we don't let her in until she gets something else."

"Well, you're a crab tonight," Boggs said, sitting next to her. "What's up? Not getting any?"

Vicky punched Boggs on the arm. "You're such an ass." She looked at Toni and shrugged. She had an apologetic look on her face. "Sorry. I guess I am a little edgy. I just can't figure out what this maniac is going to do next. And I don't want anyone else to have to die for us to figure this out."

Toni went over and gave Vicky a hug. "I know, sweetie. This is getting to all of us. Maybe after we eat we can go over what we know and something will click."

"I hope so." Vicky finished the rest of her beer. "Damn. Seeing you two makes me wish Claire didn't work the night shift. I hardly ever get to see her."

Toni sat at one of the kitchen stools. Mr. Rupert was still sitting in the one next to Vicky. She rubbed his head and laughed. "It looks like Mr. Rupert is waiting for food along with us."

"I'll feed the boys before Patty gets here so they'll leave us alone," Boggs said. She got out a can of wet food and divided it onto two plates. Mr. Rupert hopped up on the counter to eat. Boggs took the other plate to Little Tuffy, who was waiting patiently on one of the ottomans. She waited until they finished, about seventeen seconds, then put their plates in the dishwasher.

"You guys are so cute," Vicky said.

Toni expected an additional sarcastic remark, but Vicky remained silent.

"Jeez, Vic, you're serious aren't you?"

"Actually I am." She took a sip of her fresh beer. "All this crap has made me realize how short life really is. I want what you guys have," she added softly.

Toni scooted over to the stool Mr. Rupert had vacated. She put her arm around Vicky and squeezed. "Do you love her, Vic?"

Vicky lowered her head and sighed. She was quiet for so long that Toni almost asked her again.

"Yes," Vicky said, her voice just above a whisper. "I really do."

"Do you think she feels the same way?"

"I'm pretty sure. She tells me she loves me all the time. It's just hard to believe that someone like her would love someone like me, that's all."

"I feel the same way about Boggs," Toni said. "I have a hard time believing it."

"Are you nuts?" Boggs asked. "It's the other way around. I'm the one who lucked out."

"See what I mean?" Vicky said. "You guys really love each other and you get to spend all your off time together."

"Are you thinking of asking Claire to move in with you?" Toni asked.

"I'm afraid to. What if she says no?"

"I know exactly how you feel," Boggs said. "I was terrified that Toni would say no, or worse, that she would laugh at me."

"Really?" Toni couldn't believe that Boggs had felt that way.

"Yeah, I did. But I figured it was worth taking the chance."

She took another sip of beer and smiled at Toni. "Cuz I love you so much." She put her hand on Vicky's shoulder. "If you love her, take the chance, Vic. Believe me, it's totally worth it."

"If I thought I could be half as happy as you guys, I'd do it. I'm, uh, really considering it. I've been talking to your Aunt Francie." Vicky was almost blushing.

"You're thinking of buying a place?" Boggs asked. Her aunt was a realtor.

"Yeah. I've been living in my tiny apartment for eight years now," she continued. "The landlord has never raised my rent, but then again he's never done a damn thing to fix the place either. Anyway, he said a few months ago that he was going to sell the building, so I started kind of looking around. I've saved enough money for a good down payment, plus enough to start fixing a place up."

"That's wonderful," Toni said. "What about Claire? Does she rent or own a place?"

"She rents a small place across from the hospital," Vicky said. "She's been living there since she was a resident."

"Where are you looking?" Boggs asked.

"Actually, Francie showed me a place only a block from here. It's not quite as big as this place, and obviously not rehabbed like yours, but it has good bones. And I'm pretty handy at doing some of the work myself. And Claire said she likes to do things like that. We talked about it once, kind of hypothetically."

"We can help you do painting and stuff," Toni said. "Have you made an offer?"

"Not yet, but I think I'm going to. Even if I don't ask Claire to move in with me. With the way the market is right now, I think this is a good time to buy."

"Oh, I agree," Toni said. "The perfect time."

"And Aunt Francie is good," Boggs added. "She'll be able to tell you how low you can bid."

Vicky's eyes seemed to brighten. "I think I will. I need something positive to focus on." She pulled out her phone and dialed. After a short conversation she closed her phone. "Francie said she'd have the paperwork ready for me in the morning. She thinks I can offer a lot less than I expected."

Toni hugged her again. "This is fabulous, hon. When are you going to talk to Claire?"

Vicky took a long drink from her beer. "One thing at a time, okay?" She grinned. "But it sure would be nice if we could be working on it together."

The doorbell rang.

"Hey, don't tell them yet, okay?" Vicky asked. "I don't want to jinx anything."

"Got it," Boggs said as she got up to answer the door.

"I hope you don't have Subs R Us," Vicky yelled as Patty and Johnnie entered the foyer.

"We stopped at the pet store and got dog food," Johnnie replied as they came around the corner to the kitchen. She was carrying two reusable grocery bags.

"Good one," Boggs said, chuckling.

Patty laughed. "We stopped at that new grocery store down the street," she said as she started to unload the bags. "They have a fantastic deli there. Have you guys tried it?"

"Anne talked about it yesterday," Toni said as she peered into one of the bags. "It sure smells good."

Boggs was getting out plates for everyone. "Who wants beer?"

"We do," Patty said as she began opening the containers. "We got a little bit of everything just to try it. Here's some potato salad, chicken tenders, lasagna, mac and cheese, hot wings, scalloped potatoes and some ham."

"Holy crap, Patty," Boggs said. "Were you guys hungry or something?" She took a forkful of the potato salad. "This is pretty good," she said with her mouth still full.

They filled their plates and ate quickly, as though they hadn't had a meal in days. Toni licked the hot sauce off her fingers and pushed her plate away. "Jeez, I'm stuffed. Thanks for the great food, you guys."

"It's not that I would go there every day," Patty said. "But it's damn good."

"Yeah," Johnnie agreed. "Now I can bring some actual food for Thanksgiving."

Toni laughed. "I think we've got it covered. Just stick with your original plan of soda and beer. You all ready to go downstairs?"

They cleaned up the remaining food, got fresh drinks and headed down to the game room. Johnnie sat at the end of the bar, took out her laptop and lit a cigarette. Patty sat next to her. Toni and Boggs sat on one end of the sectional couch and Vicky took the other side with Mr. Rupert.

"First off," Toni began, "I had an interesting talk with Judge Crayton today." She recounted their conversation.

"That's interesting," Boggs said. "I already think that Peter is a slimeball, and I knew I didn't like the mayor. But I was just thinking the mayor was a bigot, not necessarily doing something illegal."

"I trust the judge's instincts," Toni said. "But I have no idea how the mayor could make trouble for us."

"I'm not sure either," Vicky said. "But when I was digging into all that crap about dirty lawyers and judges a few months ago, the mayor's name came up a couple of times. He's just the kind of religious idiot that probably diddles with little boys or something. I could never find anything solid on him, but it was just a feeling, you know? At least it's nice to know that we have some decent folks on our side. The judge, Anne Mulhoney and Captain Billings."

Vicky's phone rang and she glanced at the name. "Speak of the devil. It's Captain Billings." She listened mostly and gave short replies. "I understand, Captain. Okay, we'll keep you updated." She closed her phone. "He says that no one came around Amy's room today and he has to release the body now. Guess our guy didn't care. And Captain Billings said the mayor is going to give a press conference at seven tonight. It will be on Channel Eleven."

"What the hell for?" Boggs asked.

"Apparently he's going to reassure us peons that *his* police department will get to the bottom of these home invasions or else he'll find replacements."

"What an ass," Boggs replied.

"It's almost seven now," Toni said. She picked up the remote from the coffee table and turned on the television.

Vicky scooted to the other side of the couch next to Boggs so she could see the screen. Johnnie and Patty could see from where they were. They watched as the mayor gave his press conference. It was more like a sermon, but he made his point. Toni hit the mute button when it was over.

"Funny how he seemed most upset about Joshua Andrews, the widower and loving father of two wonderful children." Vicky's face was red with anger. "He barely mentioned Linda, and she was a city firefighter for God's sake."

"And did you see that giant cross around his neck?" Johnnie asked. "Could he find a bigger one?"

"And what was all that crap about him knowing Mr. Andrews?" Boggs asked. "I bet you he never met the guy. There's no way he was feeling a personal loss. No way."

"I think Mr. Andrews was on some planning committee," Johnnie said. She keyed in a search on her laptop. "Yeah," she said a minute later. "He was on the park committee and I bet that's how the mayor met him. But I'm betting he never did more than pass him in City Hall."

"We all know he's a pompous ass and a bigot," Toni said. "And that he makes no bones about it. The fact that he says he *tolerates* gays says it all. I'm still not sure how he's going to cause trouble for us. But for now, let's try to focus on our maniac here. See if we can find something we missed. I'm positive it's right in front of us, but we're just not seeing it." She couldn't shake the feeling that she was close to figuring out the missing piece.

They spent the next two hours going over the information they'd already gathered and tried to make some sense of it all.

He watched the news conference with his mother and felt his jaw clench when the mayor finished talking. *Hypocrite.* How could he say that he was friends with that deviant man? A man who proudly claimed to be the father of a deviant? He excused himself, twisting his ring as he walked. He needed the calm of his sanctuary.

He sat at his desk and tried to pray, but his anger and confusion clouded his thoughts. He had always thought that the mayor was a pious and righteous man, believing the same as he. He'd even campaigned for the mayor in his reelection last spring and attended the morning prayer meetings. He thought he knew the mayor, but now he just felt betrayed. His mission was for the good of all God-fearing people in the United States, and the mayor had said it was shameful that the deviant had been killed. *It's you who are shameful, allowing deviants to work in the police department and fire department.* He felt his heart race as his fury grew and realized he was grinding his teeth. He took several deep breaths.

Once his breathing slowed, he dropped to his knees and prayed for guidance. The mayor had vowed to stop the killings and he couldn't let that happen. Not now, not ever. It wasn't time. His list wasn't complete.

He stilled his mind and waited for an answer. It didn't take long. God spoke to him clearly. Now he just needed a plan. A way to complete this task. And it would be a wonderful accomplishment, to silence the betrayer. It would be like silencing Judas. He smiled.

He rose from his knees and sat at his desk. He would need a little more information. "The Internet is a blessed thing," he said quietly. It took him less than fifteen minutes to find out everything he needed to know. He knew God would help him.

He spent twenty minutes typing out his mission and his beliefs. He knew if this didn't end well, he wanted everyone to know about the great things he'd done for the country. He saved the document on a zip drive and slipped it in his pocket. He took his gym bag with him and paused in the living room. "I need to run an errand, Mother. Is there anything I can bring back for you?"

She smiled at him. "I baked some cookies today, but we're low on milk. Could you bring home some?"

He kissed her on the cheek, as he always did. "Yes. I'll be back within the hour."

He drove to the corner gas station and went to the pay phone on the side. The streetlight was burned out and he stood in the shadows of the building as he made the call to the mayor. He was pretty sure this was the mayor's home number, but he wasn't positive. He felt anxious until he heard a woman's soft voice answer the phone. Ah, the wife, he thought. She'll be better off now that the betrayer is about to be cast out along with his deviant associates.

He altered his voice only slightly and asked to speak to the mayor. Once the mayor came to the phone, he began his story. He told the mayor he was a fellow member and had information about the killings. The unfortunate thing, he'd said, was that it was a good Christian who has realized the error of his ways. And, he continued, it was a member of the mayor's own staff.

"He has asked me to talk to you," he said, his voice still disguised. "He wants your forgiveness before he turns himself in. And he has some sort of computer thing to give you. I think he called it a thumb drive. He said he'd deleted it from his computer at work, but that you should have the information."

There was silence on the other end and he feared that the mayor wasn't going to fall for his plan. "Are you still there?"

"Yes." The mayor's voice was much quieter than it had been at the beginning. There was another long pause. "Where?"

He smiled. Not only was the mayor a Judas, he was obviously doing something else that was either illegal or immoral. The message he'd received from God was right, of course. The mayor was dirty. He gave a location to the mayor, indicating that he'd be there with the killer in fifteen minutes.

He got back in his car and waited. He knew that if things didn't go well, they'd find the zip drive in his pocket. He didn't want there to be any doubt that God had spoken directly to him and that he was God's special messenger. He said another prayer and headed off to the meeting spot.

The mayor's car was already there, parked in an alley behind a warehouse. He'd circled the block and did not detect any police officers, but he couldn't be sure. He pulled his car up next to the mayor's, their driver's side windows together. He rolled down his window and watched as the mayor did the same.

"Hello, Judas," he said. He could see his breath in the cold night air.

He thought the mayor looked momentarily confused, then terrified as he saw the muzzle of his nine-millimeter gun. This time it sounded much louder than a firecracker, probably because it was inside his car. It only took one shot, and the mayor slumped. He pulled out a Bible from his gym bag and tossed it inside the car. He hesitated for a moment, wondering if he should use the myrrh oil, but decided against it. He didn't want to touch this man, this betrayer of God. He looked straight ahead and drove away, stopping at the convenience store for milk.

Toni was getting herself another beer when Vicky's phone rang.

"It's Captain Billings again," Vicky said. After a few one-word answers, she closed her phone. "The mayor's been shot. He's dead. It's probably our guy. He left a Bible." She filled them in on the details she knew.

"What the hell?" Toni was confused. The mayor was known for his conservative values and he was a member of The Fellowship. Why would the maniac target the mayor when they seemed to share the same distorted views, she wondered.

"Are we going to the scene?" Patty asked.

"Captain Billings has the same crime scene unit there and he's already talked to the mayor's wife himself. He said that she told him the mayor got a call and then went out. He didn't tell her where he was going. He's got a dump on the phone."

"So our guy was somehow able to lure the mayor out." Toni tapped her finger on her lips. "But why? It must have something to do with the press conference."

"I wish we could watch it again," Patty said. "Maybe we missed something."

"Hey!" Boggs grabbed the remote. "I had the DVR set to record that game show at seven."

"You watch game shows?" Johnnie asked, snickering.

"Yes, I do. That stupid one where they have to jump through a hole. It cracks me up." She found the show and hit play. "The press conference was only about ten minutes long," she said.

They stared at the television and watched the entire thing again. No one said a word. When it was over, Boggs stopped the recording.

"I didn't hear anything," Johnnie said.

"The only thing that stood out to me was the fact that he felt a *personal* loss regarding Mr. Andrews," Toni said.

"Which was total bullshit," Boggs added.

Toni nodded. "Okay, let's assume that our maniac watched the press conference."

"But why would he be so pissed at the mayor?" Patty asked. "I mean, the mayor said he'd get to the bottom of this, do you think that's what set him off?"

"I don't think so," Toni said. "He would expect the mayor to say that. We all did. The only thing that surprised any of us was the bit about Mr. Andrews."

"I'm not sure I follow you," Patty said. "Is it just me?"

"Me, either," Johnnie said.

Vicky shrugged.

"Okay, here's what I'm thinking," Toni continued. "And it's just a guess. But like I said, we all expected the mayor to say he'd do what he could to stop the murders. Our killer might think that the mayor was just saying what he needed to say. Just like us. Does that make sense?"

Everyone nodded. "In other words," Patty said, "the maniac assumed the mayor would say that even though he secretly agreed that the killings were a good thing?"

"Exactly," Toni replied. "But I think it pissed our guy off when the mayor seemed genuinely upset about Mr. Andrews."

"Oh, I get it," Boggs chimed in. "That would look like the mayor approved of Mr. Andrews, right?"

"Yes, I think so." Toni took a sip of her beer. "Everyone in Fairfield knows that the mayor is a bigoted asshole and that he's a mile right of conservatives." She shook her head. "How the hell did he get elected anyway?"

"Because the Democrat running against him died," Vicky reminded her.

"Oh, that's right. Anyway, when the mayor acted like he was a personal friend of Mr. Andrews, that must have thrown our guy for a loop. He might have even felt betrayed by someone who believed the same as he did. That's my best guess right now."

They talked about the possibilities.

Vicky's phone rang again. "It's Captain Billings again." She talked for several minutes, then closed her phone. "He said that the call to the mayor came from a pay phone. He sent some uniforms over there and no one saw a damned thing. It's on the side of a gas station. There aren't any cameras there. We've got squat."

"I don't suppose the mayor's wife knew anything?" Johnnie asked.

"No, not as far as I know," Vicky said. "We're no closer now than we were after the first murder. Damn it." She slammed her beer bottle down on the coffee table. "Oh, jeez. I'm sorry."

"No worries, sweetie," Toni said. "We're all a little on edge."

"We've got three good suspects, but no evidence," Vicky said. "We've only got the last three on a license plate and our gut feelings. That's not enough to question any of them. I don't want them to know we're looking at them."

"Especially not Peter," Boggs added. "He'd bolt for sure."

"I'm leaning toward Peter as our guy," Johnnie said. "Mostly because of the evidence, or lack thereof. I think he's showing his badge to get in. And he knows enough not to leave anything behind. Plus there's the whole Fellowship thing. If we could only figure out how he's getting the insulin."

"That seems to be a big key," Vicky said. "But there's no way to find out who is getting it. Claire talked to her supervisor and she said that the hospital isn't missing any."

"We know that Mevin is a diabetic," Patty added. "But it doesn't seem likely that he's using his own insulin. He'd get really sick, wouldn't he?"

"Yeah, he would," Vicky said. "Damn it. What are we missing? Let's go over this again. We have Joe Jackson the creepy neighbor, Mevin Murran the defrocked nurse with a bad temper, and Peter Johnson the asshole." She flipped open her notebook. "The only thing we know for sure is that each one of them has, or has access to, a dark colored Ford van with the last three on the plates being six, six, six."

"We know that the only way Peter got his job was through the mayor," Boggs added. "Who is now dead. I can see Peter doing that. And the mayor would definitely meet with Peter, don't you think?"

"True," Toni said. "But wouldn't the mayor's wife have recognized his voice?"

"Yeah, I guess you're right," Boggs said. "Unless the son of a bitch disguised his voice."

"Instead of trying to place one of these guys at a scene, why don't we try to eliminate one of them?" Patty said. "Maybe that would be easier."

"Well, Peter and Joe work during the day and all the murders took place in the evening," Vicky said. "Except for Linda." She blinked back tears. "Hers was in the late afternoon."

"Maybe we can check Mevin's schedule at Christian Hospital?" Johnnie said. "He does shifts, so maybe he was at work when one of the murders happened. It seems unlikely that he could leave in the middle of his shift and get back without someone noticing."

"I can do that," Vicky said. "At least it's something."

Toni sighed, then reached for her now empty beer. She looked at the bottle and set it back down.

"Do you want another one, babe?" Boggs asked. "Anyone?"

Toni shook her head. The others also declined.

"I just feel like I'm missing something obvious and it's driving me nuts," Toni said. "I'm positive this guy is working on two lists, just like Cathy said. Linda and the mayor are definitely on the second list. Maybe this list is more personal to him. He shot them and didn't do the stun gun or stoning thing. Maybe Linda either did something or represented something that pissed him off. Same with the mayor. The others seem to be on a different kind of list. I'm just not understanding what it is, but I know it is very important to him."

Vicky glanced at her watch. "I don't think there's anything else we can do tonight," she said. "I think I'll stop by the mayor's house and give my condolences to his wife."

Johnnie raised her eyebrows at that comment.

"In other words, I want to see what she knows," Vicky said. "I know that Captain Billings already talked to her, but I just want to get a feel for her." She stood. "And Claire is getting off a little early tonight," she added. "I want to make sure I have enough time to get ready."

"Enough said," Boggs replied with a grin.

"Patty and I are going to head out also," Johnnie said, draining the rest of her beer. "She's beating me at Detective Firebrand."

Toni and Boggs walked them out and locked the doors behind them. Boggs made sure the alarm was set and double-checked all the doors. "I'm getting a bad feeling about all this," she said quietly. "We usually know more than this. I feel like we're completely in the dark."

"I know. Me, too. But it's hard to figure out what's going on in the mind of a crazy person. They don't do what you expect them to do. You almost have to think crazy to even get a clue."

While Boggs got the coffee ready for the morning, Toni grabbed a bottle of water and sat at the island. Mr. Rupert sat next to her.

Boggs seemed to notice her frustration. "Hey, babe. Why don't we make a list of what we have to do before Thanksgiving? And I guess we need to start a grocery list."

Toni smiled and retrieved a pad of paper and pencil from the island drawer. Boggs knew her well. She always felt better if she could make a list. Any kind of list. She routinely made lists for cleaning the house, grocery lists and Christmas card lists. "Let me grab the Thanksgiving food list from my briefcase," she said excitedly. "I'll redo it and then we can see if there's anything we're missing."

Her briefcase was in the mudroom and she quickly retrieved the crumpled piece of paper. She sat back down at the island and started a fresh list. She handed the old one to Boggs, who was now sitting next to her with a bottle of lemon water. "Here, you read off what we have so far."

Boggs started to read off the items.

"Wait," Toni said. "I need a bigger pad of paper." She pulled out a legal pad from the drawer. Boggs gave her a puzzled look. "I need to divide everything up, you know, main dishes, sides, desserts. And I need room to put down who's bringing what."

Boggs chuckled and waited for her to make the different headings on her list. "Okay, I'm ready."

They went through the old list, then stared at the huge list of food.

"I think we'll be able to feed the entire neighborhood," Boggs said.

Toni laughed. "And Mom thought we wouldn't have enough. I think we've got everything covered. We'll need to get out the turkeys from the freezer tomorrow and put them in the fridge. The ham too. Okay, let's start our grocery list. I think we should go on either Monday night or Tuesday night after work. It will be a zoo on Wednesday."

Boggs took the small pad of paper and began writing. "I'll need two heads of cauliflower and sharp cheddar for my casserole." She jotted those items down. "I wonder if I have enough bread crumbs."

Toni hopped down and checked the pantry. She was feeling wonderful. Even though there was a maniac out there, she was safe at home with the woman she loved. And here they were, getting ready for their first Thanksgiving dinner. She was overcome with emotion and wiped away a tear. She opened the door to the pantry and looked on the shelves. "You've got an unopened can here," she informed Boggs. "And we only have one can of turkey broth. Better put that on the list."

"What about cream of chicken soup? We both need that for our casseroles."

"We only have one can." She picked up a box of Minute Rice and shook it. "And put rice on the list."

"What about the stuff for stuffing?" Boggs asked. She laughed. "Stuff for stuffing."

"Mom said she was bringing that," Toni replied. "And the ingredients for dressing."

"What the hell is the difference?"

"One is fixed on the stove top or in the turkey and the other in the oven," Toni said. "I don't like either, so I really don't have any idea. Do you like stuffing?"

"I like to eat it once," Boggs answered. "But I'm not wild about it. It's just something I think you should eat on turkey day."

"Oh, I almost forgot. Put down a can of pumpkin. And eggs. We'll need eggs."

Boggs looked at the menu list. "I thought Sam and Betty were bringing pumpkin pie?"

"They are," Toni said. "But I'm making pumpkin chiffon pie. Better put fake piecrust on the list."

Boggs scratched her head. "Okay, first, what the hell is fake piecrust? And second, what's the difference between pumpkin pie, which I hate, and pumpkin whatever pie?"

Toni laughed out loud. She came out of the pantry and hugged Boggs. "God, I love you! I'm getting fake piecrust because no one can make piecrust like my mom, so why bother. You can get them frozen and you just add the insides. As for the difference, regular pumpkin pie is kind of dense, and I don't like it either. Pumpkin chiffon is light and fluffy. You beat egg whites and blend them in. Oh, that reminds me. Add Cool Whip to the list."

Boggs did as instructed. "So it's not heavy and grainy? The pie you make?"

"No, not at all. I'm with you. I can't stand regular pumpkin pie. Or pumpkin anything for that matter."

"Okay, I'll try a bite of yours then." She smiled. "This is going to be so much fun. A lot of work, but a lot of fun. Having all our favorite people over and everything. I've never had a family holiday at a place of my own. Have you?"

Toni thought for a moment. She'd been with her ex for almost seven years, but they'd never hosted a holiday. "Nope. This is a first for me too. I'm glad it's you and me."

Boggs kissed her. "We do make a good team, don't we?"

"Yes, we do. The best team *ever*. Let's finish our lists and go to bed."

"And pick up where we left off?"

"Absolutely!"

They made a few adjustments to their menu and finished the grocery list. Then they discussed seating and decided they definitely needed help in that department. Toni didn't want to send people to the basement to eat, so they'd need to borrow and beg for tables and chairs.

"How many people will be here?" Boggs asked.

Toni looked at her guest list. "Holy cow. Including us there will be sixteen people. Aunt Doozie and Uncle Tom aren't coming into town until Friday, so we don't have to count them. How in the world are we going to fit everyone in here?"

Boggs looked at the living room area. "Well, we have enough room, just nowhere to sit. Aunt Francie has a nice table and chairs we could probably borrow. The table folds, but it's pretty sturdy. I'll call her tomorrow. What about your folks? Do they have a card table or something?"

"Yeah, they've got a really nice one I'm sure we could borrow. But that still leaves us short."

"We could bring up the game table and chairs from the basement," Boggs suggested. "We could take the big ottomans downstairs and that will give us extra room." She thought for a moment. "I think we should buy our own table and chairs," she said. "We'll run into this same problem again, so why not?"

"That could be pretty expensive," Toni said.

Boggs rolled her eyes. "I think we can afford it, babe. Anyway, we'll use it over and over. We don't have a real dining area, so if we ever have more than three other people over, we're screwed."

"I guess you're right," Toni agreed.

"Let's go upstairs and check online and see what we can find. We can go out tomorrow and shop." Boggs pulled her off the stool. "Come on. It'll be fun."

They scooted the two office chairs close together and sat in front of Boggs's computer. They tried several local stores.

"Everything is so expensive," Toni complained. "And we can't really have a normal table because there's nowhere to store it when we're not using it."

"Hmm. Let's try a different kind of search. Let's put in convertible furniture." Boggs keyed in several things and they looked at the results. "Look," she said pointing to the screen. "This would be perfect. It folds down to be a sofa table, but can seat six people."

"How cool is that? And the price isn't too bad," Toni said.

"I think we should get two," Boggs said. "We can keep one in the living room and put the other in the storage room when we're not having a giant dinner party. Now let's look for chairs."

After a few more searches, they were able to find chairs that looked like regular dining chairs, but folded for easy storage. "Hey look," Boggs said. "If we order online, we get free shipping. It says if we order by midnight, it will be delivered on Wednesday. We're both off that day, so it will be perfect. We'll get two of these tables and how many chairs?"

"Are you sure?" Toni asked.

"Absolutely. This is a great deal and we'll use them for years. So how many chairs should we get? Ten?"

"Well, if the tables each sit six, we should get twelve," Toni said.

"Duh, that's right." Boggs added twelve chairs to her cart and two tables. "Do you want anything else?"

"I think we've done enough shopping for one night," Toni

said.

Boggs was busy shopping in other departments. "Let's see what they have in their clearance section," she said. "You never know." She looked at her watch. "We've got a little less than two hours to shop, so we'll get the delivery date." She chuckled.

"Then look at the clearance shoes," Toni said. "See if they have anything fun."

Boggs laughed. "Yeah, you really *need* some new shoes."

Toni laughed. "I don't know what's gotten into me this past year. I've become a real shoe whore. Before that I never owned more than maybe four pairs of shoes at a time. I can't help myself. But almost all of them were on sale." It was a weak attempt to justify her enormous collection of shoes. "Wait! Go back."

Boggs hit the button.

"Look at those red tennies. And they're seventy percent off!"

"And you only have what, three pairs of red shoes?"

"Not like these," Toni argued. "These are adorable. And for less than eight dollars? Who could pass up that?"

Boggs added the shoes to her cart.

"Okay," Toni said. "I've gotten my treat. Why don't you look in the gadgets department? I'm sure you could use some type of computer thingy."

"Touché," Boggs said. "You have your shoes and I have computer *thingys*. But I'd rather have some more spy stuff. That Big Ear the gang gave us is a real hoot. You really can hear people talk. But I don't think this store has any of that stuff. Let's just go ahead and order. Maybe we can go to a spy store tomorrow since we don't have to look for a table and chairs."

"Sounds good. And I don't need those shoes, sweetie. Go ahead and delete that. I already have enough red ones."

"Okay, I'll just order the table and chairs," Boggs said.

"Agreed," Toni said. "You finish up here and I'll get ready for bed." She kissed Boggs's neck. "Hurry up, hon."

Boggs cupped Toni's face in her hands and kissed her passionately. "I'll be in there as soon as I do this."

Toni felt her knees get a little weak. *After over a year, how can one kiss still do that to me?* She went down to their bedroom and got ready for Boggs.

# Chapter 17

The weekend passed quickly for Toni. She and Boggs had raked leaves and jumped in the piles. They grilled burgers on Saturday evening and added slices of Swiss cheese logs to the top. It was an experiment that turned out fabulous. On Sunday, they watched football and snuggled on the couch. They never talked about the maniac and only heard from Vicky once. She'd called to say that she had put in an offer on the house and that the deadline for acceptance was Monday afternoon.

When Toni got to work on Monday morning, she felt rested and excited about Thanksgiving. It had felt good to take a break from the reality of what was happening. Her calendar was light for both today and tomorrow and she was grateful. The only thing she had today in court was one motion hearing. She pulled out her file and started to do some research, checking the case law that the defense attorney had cited. She jumped when her phone buzzed.

"Yes?"

"Good morning, Ms. Barston," Chloe said pleasantly. "There's a Mr. Charlie Jones on line two for you. He says it's urgent."

"Ugh." She debated about whether or not to take his call. *Might as well get it over with because he'll just keep calling and leaving messages for me if I don't.* "Okay, Chloe. I'll take it. Thank you."

She took a deep breath before hitting the button. She was so disgusted with how he treated Vicky and anyone else that was gay. *But he just gives me the creeps. He's so pathetic.* What happened to not judging people, she told herself. I'm judging him because he's so judgmental. She laughed at the absurdity of it all and punched line two.

"Good morning, Charlie. How are you today?" Toni surprised herself at how sincere she sounded, and actually felt.

"Fine, Toni," he said. "But I have some very important information for you. I think I know where to find evidence on Frank."

"Shouldn't you give that information to the police?" Toni asked. "I can't really do anything but pass it along."

"I know," Charlie said, "but this implicates someone else, too. Maybe even has something to do with the murder of the mayor. I really think you should see for yourself. I trust you. Maybe I'm just blowing this all out of proportion. But you were a therapist before. Anyway, I can't really go into it on the phone. Can you meet me?"

*What the hell?* I guess it makes sense to want to talk to me, she thought. He won't talk to Vicky. Maybe he knows something about Mevin. *Crap.* She couldn't decide what to do.

"Are you still there?" Charlie asked.

"Yes, I'm sorry. I was just looking at my calendar." She didn't feel like meeting him today.

"It's really important," Charlie continued. "Maybe tomorrow then?"

She felt a little relieved, thinking that she could put the meeting off for another day. "Okay, tomorrow at about two? Do you want me to come over to Help Services?"

"No. I don't want anyone to see us talking," he said. "I don't want any of the guys to think I broke their confidentiality or anything."

"That makes sense," Toni said. "Where do you want to meet?"

"How about at Jeff's Diner on Third Street?" he suggested. "It won't be crowded at all that time of day."

"Okay, I'll meet you at two tomorrow." She hung up and jotted it down on her calendar. *What the hell kind of information does he have? Should I have agreed to meet him today?* She shrugged and got back to her research.

Shortly before the end of the day, Toni's mom called to check on the status of Thanksgiving dinner. Toni assured her that everything was under control and that they would have plenty of food. Her mom informed her that she'd added a couple more items to her own list and then started laughing.

"What's so funny, Mom?"

"Oh, it's your father. I don't know why he listens to that woman on the radio. He just yells at her."

"Which woman is that?"

"Oh, Doctor Nancy I think her name is. But she's no doctor, that's for sure. She's the one that says every answer is in the Bible."

Toni took her attention off her computer screen. "What did you say?"

"I said she's no doctor," her mother said. "She's a quack."

"No, after that. Something about the Bible?"

"Yes. She thinks that the answer to everything, including hemorrhoids, is right there in the Bible. Now that's what I call a liberal interpretation."

"Tell Dad to keep yelling. I've got to run now, Mom. I'll talk to you tomorrow. I love you."

Toni hung up the phone. *It can't be that simple, can it?* She tried to remember, but couldn't. She tapped her fingers on her desk. *The Internet!* She keyed in a search, found what she was looking for and hit print. She rushed out of her office and grabbed the

166

paper from the printer. *Holy shit.*

"Boggs!" She saw her at the end of the hall, chatting with a uniformed cop. She was very excited, but she tried to act calm and professional.

Boggs must have sensed the urgency in her voice, because she began walking very quickly. "What's going on? Are you okay?"

"I think I figured out the list. Look at this." She shoved the paper into her hands.

"I don't get it." Boggs looked at her then back at the list.

Toni pointed to the first and second entry. Then ran her finger down the list and pointed to the eighth entry. When Boggs shook her head, indicating she still didn't understand, Toni said, "Amy Judge."

"Holy crap. Holy crap."

"And look at the next one," Toni said. "Ruth. How much you want to bet it will be Harriet Ruth?"

"Harriet from Stray Rescue?"

Toni nodded.

Boggs pulled out her phone.

"Tell Vicky and everyone to meet us there," Toni said as she ran back to her office. She quickly grabbed her briefcase and jacket and met Boggs in the hall. They almost ran to the elevator.

"Vicky is sending units there," Boggs said, still on the phone. "She called using someone else's phone and no one is answering." Boggs listened to Vicky as they waited for the elevator. "Okay, we're on our way." She looked at Toni. "She's going to call Patty and have her check out her house. But do you mind if I drive?"

Toni handed her the keys while they were in the elevator to the garage. "Yeah, we'll get there quicker if you drive."

"How did you figure it out?"

"My mom said something about the answer being in the Bible and it just hit me."

"I hope we're in time."

The elevator door opened and they ran to Toni's VW Bug.

They'd been driving only about five minutes when Boggs's cell phone rang. She pulled it out, glanced at caller ID and handed it to Toni.

"What's going on?" Toni asked.

"The shelter is closed today, but there was a girl inside. Everything is fine here, but no Harriet. Patty is almost to her house."

"Should we go there," Toni asked. "Where does she live?"

"No," Vicky said. "One way or another, there's nothing you guys could do anyway."

Toni relayed the information to Boggs, who slowed her driving. "Then what the hell should we do?" Boggs asked, obviously frustrated.

"I heard that," Vicky said. "Go to your place and start looking at our list. See if that's the only Ruth on there. As soon as we know anything, we'll call you. Then we'll meet you there. If she's dead, then I'll turn it over to the crime scene guys. If she's okay, we'll put her in protective custody or something."

"Okay," Toni said. "I guess you're right. She can stay with us if she wants. We've got plenty of room."

"I'll let you know." Vicky disconnected.

Both Toni and Boggs kept shaking their heads all the way home.

They'd barely gotten inside when Patty called.

"Harriet is fine," Patty said. "I found her at her girlfriend's house. She's been staying there the last couple of nights. That might have been what saved her."

"Does she want to come here?" Toni asked.

"I told her, but she wants to stay with her girl. Who can blame her? But we're going to keep a uniform there, just in case. We'll be over in a few. Johnnie is picking up food for us."

Toni hung up the phone. "Let's go up and change out of our work clothes," she said. She filled in Boggs on the way up.

After they had changed into jeans and sweatshirts, Boggs slipped her pancake holster onto her waistband. She opened Toni's nightstand and pulled out Toni's gun. "Here, babe. I'd feel better if you were carrying also. Not that anything is going to happen in our house, but in case we need to run out fast. Okay?"

Toni nodded. She too felt better with having her own protection. She wasn't used to having a gun on her, but she was more than familiar with using one. She'd demonstrated her expertise at the shooting range months ago. And in fact, she was a better shot than any of the others. But even though she could shoot better, she didn't have the experience the others did. And adrenaline did strange things to a person.

They went back downstairs and opted for soda instead of beer. "Even though I could use a cold beer," Toni said, "I think we need to keep a clear head."

Toni pulled out the paper she'd printed at work and compared it to the list from Fairfield Human Rights Organization. She was still looking at the names when the rest of the gang arrived. They joined her at the kitchen island.

"Did you find anyone?" Vicky asked.

"Not yet," Toni said.

Patty had her own list. "I'll start at the bottom. I wish they were in alphabetical order."

Johnnie had stopped and gotten fried chicken and set the food on the island. No one ate. They just watched the two women pore over the list.

"I think I've got it," Toni said. "Here." She pointed to the name. "Rose Samuel. Here's her address and phone number."

Vicky leaned over and began dialing her phone. "Patty, call this in and have a uniform go over there." After several minutes of a somewhat vague explanation to Rose Samuel, Vicky closed her phone. "She doesn't really understand, but she's cooperative. She agreed not to open the door unless it is a uniformed cop."

Everyone seemed to relax a bit and Toni and Boggs got plates and drinks.

"Okay," Johnnie said. "I'm a little bit out of the loop here. What's the deal?"

"He's following the books of the Bible," Toni said. "At least it looks that way." She picked up the paper she'd printed and put it in front of Johnnie. "See? The first book is Genesis and the first woman's name was Catherine Geneis. Next is Exodus and

I'm betting there's someone out there with a name that's close to that. Third is Leviticus and we've got Irene Levitch. Then Numbers and that's Maggie Numerosi. John Deutermann would be Deuteronomy and Joshua Andrews would be Joshua. Judges comes next and there's Amy Judge. Ruth is the next one and Harriet's last name is Ruth."

"Holy crap," Johnnie said. "But there are two Samuels here, two books in the Bible. Are there two on the list?"

"Nope, just the one," Patty said. "Maybe he'll move on to Kings." She scanned the list. "There's no King on here."

Boggs took a bite of chicken. "But we still don't know who it is."

"And there's his other list," Toni added. "Who knows how he's picking those? But I'm pretty sure this is how he's doing the first list."

"And we don't have a damn thing on our suspects, except that they have access to a dark color van with the plates ending with six, six, six," Vicky said. "That's not enough to get a search warrant."

"What about staking out Harriet's place?" Johnnie asked. "I'll do it. All he has to do is come to the door and I'll accidentally shoot him."

"Aside from the fact that you don't have any jurisdiction and you just can't shoot someone," Vicky began, "I sent over a uniform to stay inside with backup on the next block. If *anyone* comes near Harriet's place, we'll know about it." She turned to Toni. "Did you get the sign-out sheet from Charlie?"

"Yeah, but it's useless. There were a couple scribbles and a few legible names, but none for the times we need."

"Is Charlie still on the lookout for our Peeping Tom?"

"He sure is." Toni thought for a minute. "He didn't leave any messages for me on Friday, so I had the receptionist fax me the sheet. But he called today and wanted to meet. He said he's got information about Frank Watson and something about it implicated someone else. Maybe even the mayor."

"When are you supposed to meet with him?" Vicky asked.

"I told him tomorrow. He doesn't want to meet at the clinic. He's afraid that one of his clients will see us talking."

"That makes sense. We don't want to tip off Mevin," Patty said.

"Do you think I should call him and move up the time?"

"I don't think so," Vicky said. "All he knows is that we're looking for a Peeping Tom. I doubt he's got real info on the mayor."

"Yeah, I bet you're right," Toni said. "I wish I didn't have to meet him at all. He makes me sick."

"How do you think I feel?" Vicky added. "He won't even give me the time of day."

The gang nibbled at the food, but mostly sat in silence. It seemed they were all trying to figure out what they could do to find the maniac. The sound of Vicky's phone made Toni jump.

Vicky glanced at the name on her phone and hopped off the stool. "It's personal," she called over her shoulder as she walked across the living room.

"Ah, young love," Johnnie said.

Patty hit her in the arm.

Vicky returned a few minutes later with a huge grin on her face.

"What?" Toni asked.

"I just bought myself a house!" Vicky exclaimed. "Can you believe it?"

Toni hopped off her own stool and hugged her. "That is so fabulous. When is the closing date?"

"I still have to have the inspection, but it looks like I can be in before Christmas. That would be the best present ever."

After Vicky described the house in detail, they got back to the task at hand. Again, they recounted everything they knew.

"This may sound strange," Toni began, "but something doesn't feel right."

"Well, we do have a crazy person running around," Johnnie said.

Toni rolled her eyes. "I know. But I mean that all three

suspects seem equal to me almost. Well, at least Mevin and Peter do. I'm not sure about weird Joe anymore."

"I know what you mean, babe," Boggs added. "It seems like we have the exact same information as we did at the beginning."

"Do you think Cathy could try again?" Toni asked.

Patty was already dialing her phone. "Can't hurt to ask," she said. After a short conversation, she closed her phone. "She can come over now."

When Cathy arrived, Toni started to tell her about the books in the Bible.

"No, don't tell me," Cathy said, stopping her in mid-sentence. "It works better if I don't know anything. Then I don't get in my own way." She closed her eyes for a moment, then looked back at Toni, who was sitting next to her at the island.

"I'm getting that this man feels betrayed," she began. "And that's dangerous, for all of you, but especially you, Toni."

Boggs, who had been standing, leaning against the kitchen counter, now walked over and put her hands on Toni's shoulders in a protective sort of way.

"Go on." Toni felt sick to her stomach. The same way she felt when she thought about Maggie. A wave of nausea cascaded over her body. She swallowed hard and waited for Cathy to continue.

"I see a badge," Cathy said. "He's using a badge. I don't know if it's his or not, but he's using one." She took a deep breath. "And he's planning on killing again very soon. Like in a day or two. I'm sorry, that's all I have." She looked disappointed.

"That is huge," Toni said. The nausea was lifting.

"It's got to be Peter," Boggs said. "Son of a bitch."

"I don't know what the information means," Cathy said. "I just give what I get. I hope it helps."

"More than you know," Vicky said. "Now we just have to figure out what to do."

"I wish I had more to tell you," Cathy said. "Or that I could stay, but I have to scoot. I'll see you all on Thanksgiving." She kissed Toni on the cheek. "Be careful, okay?"

Toni nodded and Boggs walked Cathy out. When she

returned, her face looked angry. "I can't believe I've worked with this guy all this time," she grunted.

"Is this enough to have him watched?" Patty asked.

Vicky was already dialing her phone. "I'm hoping Captain Billings will back us up on a hunch. We just need a couple days."

They waited while Vicky talked to the captain.

"He's going to put some of his own guys on Peter's house," Vicky said. "He said he trusted our hunches." She smiled. "Can't get a better boss than that."

"What can we do?" Patty asked.

"I'm going to let Sam in on this," Boggs said. "Is that okay?"

"Yeah, good idea," Vicky replied.

Boggs pulled out her phone and called. After relaying their information to Sam, she nodded to the group. She listened to Sam for several minutes before ringing off. "Get this," she said. "Sam said that Peter called him right after work tonight and said he needed a couple personal days. He won't be back in the office until next Monday."

"Holy crap," Vicky said. "It's got to be him." She called Captain Billings again and filled him in.

"Well, I guess I feel better about this," Toni said. "It sure sounds like it's him." "What's wrong, babe?" Boggs asked, sitting down next to her.

"It just feels like I'm still missing something." Toni knew that sounded stupid, but she couldn't shake the feeling.

"But you figured out the whole Bible book thing," Johnnie said. "Maybe that's what it was."

"I guess so," Toni said. "You're probably right." But she knew that wasn't it. There was something else. Something just didn't feel right. Something obvious that she was still missing. Maybe it's just my imagination, she thought.

The rest of the gang joked and laughed for the first time in what seemed like ages. They all seemed sure that Peter was the maniac and as soon as they nabbed him, they'd find all sorts of evidence in his house. Toni joined in, but couldn't shake the feeling. *Why did Cathy think I was in danger? If Captain Billings is having Peter watched, I'm safe, right?*

Patty and Johnnie were the first to leave. Vicky stayed back. After Boggs walked them out, she continued to sit at the island.

"What's up?" Toni asked.

"I'm trying to get up the nerve to ask Claire to move in with me," Vicky said. "I'm a nervous wreck."

Toni rubbed her shoulders. "It'll turn out fine," she said. "Does she know you put in an offer on the house?"

"No, not yet." Vicky grinned. "I was going to tell her, but I, um, guess I never did."

"Afraid of the next step?" Toni asked.

"Exactly," Vicky said. "But now that we're pretty sure it's Peter, and we've got him under surveillance, I think I feel better."

Boggs glanced at her watch. "What time does she get off?"

"She's on until eleven tonight," Vicky said. "But she's off Wednesday and Thursday. Maybe Tuesday night would be a good time. Or Thanksgiving?"

"Chicken," Boggs said. "Why not tonight?"

Vicky looked panic-stricken. "Tonight?"

"Give her a break," Toni said. "Do it whenever you think is right, Vic. Don't let her rush you."

"Maybe I could ask her tomorrow night," Vicky said. "She's going to come over to my place after she gets off work."

"That sounds perfect," Toni said. "Just perfect."

Vicky grinned, but then a frown took over her face. "What do I say? How should I ask her? I mean should I just come right out and say it? Crap."

"Just blurt it out," Boggs said. "That's the quickest way."

"Or you could give her a key," Toni suggested. "That would say it all."

Vicky relaxed a bit. "I like the key idea. Then I wouldn't have to say anything." She grinned. "Okay, gotta run. I'll talk to you guys tomorrow. I'll let you know what happens with the surveillance." She got up to leave. "You guys are working tomorrow, aren't you?"

"Yeah, we just have Wednesday off," Boggs said.

"And I'm going to meet with Charlie tomorrow," Toni said. "Ick."

"Maybe he has some decent info," Vicky said at the door. "Just pass along what he tells you, okay?"

"Will do," Toni said. "Be safe."

Boggs made sure the door was locked and the alarm was set. "Ready for bed?"

"Absolutely. This has been one long day." Toni kissed Boggs as they were standing in the foyer. "I'm glad we just have one more day, then off for five."

Boggs took her arm and led her up the stairs. "And now that they've got Peter the asshole under surveillance, we can relax a bit."

"I'm still nervous about all this," Toni said.

"We're okay, babe. Captain Billings has it under control now. Don't worry."

"Okay, I guess you're right."

But as she got ready for bed, Toni still couldn't shake the feeling. Everything made sense with Peter being the maniac, but she still thought she was missing something. What it was she had no idea. She tried to push the thoughts from her mind as she crawled into bed next to Boggs and the boys.

# Chapter 18

Toni and Boggs took separate cars to work on Tuesday. Toni needed to meet with Charlie, and Boggs had several interviews to do in the afternoon. Vicky had called before they left and informed them that Peter had not left his house all night. Somehow, that made Toni feel a little better.

She sat at her desk, doing research for her trial in two weeks. But for whatever reason, she wasn't able to concentrate. She was finished with court for the day. She gave up, closed out her research on the computer and pulled out her Thanksgiving list. It looked like they would have more than enough food, and the turkeys and ham were thawing nicely in the refrigerator. She was planning on stopping at the grocery store on the way home. There was no way in hell she was going anywhere near a grocery store on Wednesday, the day before Thanksgiving. She added a couple more things to her grocery list.

"Working hard?" Anne Mulhoney asked from the doorway.

Toni grinned as she looked up from her list. "Actually, I was adding a couple things to my grocery list," she said.

"Please don't tell me you're going tomorrow?" Anne said.

"Oh, no. I'm going after work today. It will be a total madhouse tomorrow."

"Today too," Anne said. "Do you have anything on the docket this afternoon?"

"No," Toni replied. "Do you need me to do something for you?"

"Not at all," Anne said, smiling. "Why don't you call it a day? It's almost one o'clock. Unless you rode in with Boggs."

"No, we took separate cars today," Toni said. "Are you sure?"

Anne waved her hand. "Of course. I know you're having your first Thanksgiving and there's lots to do. I almost wish Bill and I weren't having the kids over. Yours sounds more fun. The kids have lives of their own now. Not married, but we're hopeful." She smiled again.

"Well, like I said, if you want to pop over for dessert, please feel free. You don't have to call or anything," Toni said. "We'll be there stuffing ourselves all day."

"We might just do that," Anne said. "Thank you. Now get on out of here. Have a great time and I'll see you either Thursday evening or Monday morning." She left with another wave.

Toni called Boggs and told her what Anne said.

"That's great," Boggs said. "You can probably beat most of the rush at the grocery store."

"That's what I was thinking," Toni said. "Can you think of anything else we need?"

"Hmm. I don't think so. Wait. I'll stop at Sam's and get some wine and beer. It's cheaper there, okay?"

"Perfect. So I'll see you at home about when? Six?"

"Maybe earlier," Boggs said. "I've only got two more interviews to do, then I can head over to Sam's. I'll call you and let you know. Want me to pick us up something for dinner?"

"I guess so, or we can have something easy, like soup," Toni said.

"Soup sounds good to me," Boggs said. "It's kind of chilly out

177

here today. I'll see you soon, babe. I love you."

"I love you, too, sweetie." Toni smiled as she hung up the phone. She went over her list before getting ready to leave and meet Charlie.

The man had stayed home today. He didn't need to work anymore. His full-time job was his mission for God. He felt good about that. He spent most of his morning praying in his sanctuary. It was quiet and peaceful. After going through his routine, he went to work on his lists. He'd heard that the woman died in the hospital, so he was pleased with that. He could move on to the next deviant on God's list. It would be easy, just as the others had been. He twisted his ring as he thought.

He also added several more people to his personal list. This was even more fun because he could do them in whatever order he pleased. He had never felt so good, so powerful. God had chosen him, and only him, to carry out this mission. He checked his gym bag to make sure it was ready. There were five Bibles, two stones and his myrrh oil. His gun was inside, along with the silencer. He needed more insulin. He would get that out of the refrigerator in the garage on his way out. He was pleased that the insulin supply kept coming. He had contacted the company after his wife had died, telling them it was no longer needed. They'd assured him it would stop, but it never did. It came every month, regular as clockwork. Now he knew it was being sent by God.

He glanced at his watch. It was after one o'clock. He needed to make things ready. He thought about taking the zip drive with him, but decided against it. Nothing would go wrong. It never did. When it was time for him to tell the world, he would. He put the zip drive in his desk drawer and headed downstairs.

"I need to run some errands, Mother," he said, smiling.

She was sitting in her faded green recliner, watching a soap opera, as she always did in the afternoon. She waved to him and nodded, but never took her eyes off the television. He made himself a quick sandwich. I need my strength, he told himself. He sat at the kitchen table and said a prayer before eating. Fifteen minutes later he went out through the kitchen door to the garage and retrieved another vial of insulin. He smiled as he left through the back of the house. This was perfect, absolutely perfect.

Toni drove over to Jeff's Diner on Third Street. There was only one other vehicle in the parking lot. *I wonder what the food is like here.* She parked in front and waited for a couple minutes. It was only ten minutes until two. She didn't think she'd get there that quick, so she waited. It was getting cold, so she headed inside.

She had to wait a while before a waitress appeared. She looked like she was eighty years old, if she was a day.

"Just you, honey?" the old woman asked.

"I'm meeting someone," Toni said.

"What?" the woman yelled.

"I'm meeting someone," Toni yelled back.

The woman nodded and walked away.

Toni wondered if she should follow. The woman was talking, mostly to herself, so Toni hurried to catch up. The waitress stopped in front of a booth in the back.

"You want a soda or something," the waitress asked.

"Coffee would be good."

"What?" the woman yelled again.

"COFFEE." Toni shook her head. Why do people yell when they can't hear you?

The waitress disappeared and returned with an old diner mug of coffee. She spilled it as she set it on the table. She didn't seem to notice and left. Toni laughed out loud. She took a sip and decided it was one of the best cups of coffee she'd ever had. *Well, I'll be damned.* She was still enjoying the coffee when she heard the diner door open and looked up. It was Charlie. He sat across from her.

"Thanks for meeting me, Toni," he said.

"How did you ever find this place?" she asked. "The coffee is amazing."

"I know. I used to eat here when I worked a beat. I think it's the same waitress." He smiled.

The waitress appeared with another cup of coffee. "Hiya, Charlie. How's tricks?"

"Same as always, Lilly. Thanks."

She set down his mug, along with some cream and a spoon. She gave him a wink and left. Toni noticed that she didn't have a spoon, and the waitress never bothered to ask. Oh, well.

"So what did you find out?" Toni asked. She was anxious to get to the grocery store.

"I'm pretty sure that Frank is your Peeping Tom," he said. "He said some things in therapy and as an ex-cop, well, I just have a strong hunch."

"You said something about implicating someone else?" she asked. "Something about the mayor's death?"

"Yeah." He took another sip of his coffee. "And maybe I'm way off base," he continued, "but I just have a feeling. One of the other guys in therapy said something about one of the warehouses. It's close to where the mayor was killed. It seems like he keeps things there. Kind of like a lair, do you know what I mean?"

Toni shook her head. *What the hell is he talking about?*

"I think it's like a murder room. I'm not kidding." He took another sip of his coffee. "But maybe I'm just blowing it out of proportion. Hard being a therapist and a cop at the same time."

"I bet," Toni said. "That would be tough. Two completely different ways of looking at things."

"Exactly," Charlie said. "That's why I wanted you to take a look with me. The idiot gave me the keys to the place, and I think some of the stuff he has up on his walls is bizarre."

"So you've already been there?"

"Yeah, I went yesterday morning before I called you. He's out of town with his brother for Thanksgiving, so there's no worry about him coming back."

"I guess I could look," Toni said. "You said he has drawings?"

"Yeah, and they kind of spooked me. You worked with

personality disorders, right?"

"Yes," Toni said. "For several years."

"Then I think you'd be very interested in these," Charlie said. "And there's no worries about getting a search warrant since he gave me the keys. If you agree that there's something really wrong with the guy, we can call Detective Carter and have her take a look."

Toni thought for a moment. Vicky would still need to get a search warrant. Charlie couldn't give permission to have the police come inside. They'd definitely need to get a search warrant. Still, the thought of strange drawings intrigued her. "Okay, I'm game. But I only have about a half hour," she said. "I need to get back to work." *I don't want him to think I can spend all afternoon with him.*

Charlie tossed a five-dollar bill on the table. "That more than covers our coffee and tip," he said. "Do you want to leave your car here or follow me?"

"I'll just follow you so I can head right back to work. Is it far?"

"No, only a few blocks. That's why I picked Jeff's." Charlie got in his van.

Toni nodded and got in her car. *I see he's using the shelter's van. Creepy.* Now why did I think that, she asked herself. She wondered if Vicky had gotten any news about Peter yet. Surely, he would have left by now. But then again, most of the killings took place at night. The only one that didn't was Linda.

She followed him a few blocks over to a row of abandoned warehouses. He stopped in front of one and got out. He waited until she joined him. He put the key in the small door.

As Toni waited for him to unlock the door, she thought about calling Boggs, but decided against it. She was probably in the middle of an interview anyway. She followed Charlie into the building. It took a moment for her eyes to adjust to the dim light from the bright sunshine outside. She blinked several times. Something didn't feel right. She looked around and saw nothing but a large empty room.

"Where is Frank's room?" she asked.

"On the other side," Charlie said. "This is the only key I have. Come on, follow me."

He headed across the room. Toni began following him, but then it dawned on her. Everything began to make sense. She stopped dead in her tracks and felt that sense of nausea overtake her entire body.

Charlie must have realized that she'd stopped walking because he stopped and turned around. He smiled at her, but then the smile disappeared. He was only about ten feet away. He twisted his ring.

*Crap.*

Boggs relayed the information to Vicky. "Hurry, Vic."

They flew down the street and Boggs prayed that she'd get there in time. Prayed like she'd never prayed before.

He fell to his knees and prayed. It took several minutes before he could still his mind enough to pray properly. He didn't want to make God mad. His entire mission was based on *pleasing* God.

He wondered if he could have been wrong about Toni. She knew who was on the list. The list that God Himself had made. He wasn't sure whether she was one of God's children or the devil. If he made a mistake, he would be damned to hell for eternity. He had to make the right decision.

His first answer came quickly. She was not on God's list. There was no mistake about that. Her name was wrong. So he knew that he could not use the stoning on her. He frowned. He was so sure only this morning. Nothing was making sense to him. He twisted his ring and prayed some more. It took almost five solid minutes of prayer before he realized that she could be on his personal list. He needed to ask her just a few questions and he'd know for sure. Yes, this would be right. He grinned and thanked God for the confirmation.

Toni realized that she hadn't felt her phone vibrate for a while. *Does Boggs assume I'm still at the grocery store?* She began to panic. *What if they're not looking for me?* Charlie was still kneeling, and she struggled against the duct tape. Again, the nausea overtook her and she fought the urge to throw up. She couldn't budge. He'd pulled up the sleeves of her blouse and put the tape directly on her skin. It burned. She looked at the redness of her arm around the tape. *Oh, great. Who knew I was allergic to duct tape?* The absurdity of this thought made her smile.

She knew that Charlie was making his decision on how to kill her. She was pretty sure that he would kill her, just the "how" was up for grabs. She took several slow, deep breaths. The nausea was gone. She began to pray again, but not begging for rescue. This time she was thanking God for all that she'd experienced in life so far. She thanked Him for bringing Boggs into her life, for Mr. Rupert, Little Tuffy and wonderful parents. She thanked Him for her job, friends and beautiful home. She felt almost peaceful. *Is this what it's like when you're about to die?* But she didn't want to die. Not yet. So she made a conscious decision to fight as long as she could.

Charlie rose from his knees and went to Toni. He knew he'd be guided by God and he felt good about that. He knew it was almost time to tell the world all the wonderful things he'd done so far. He couldn't help but smile. They would all be so proud of him. He felt his chest fill with pride. He was God's special messenger. He took his gun out of his gym bag and slowly screwed on the silencer.

Toni tried not to change the expression on her face when she saw him with the gun. At least she wouldn't get the insulin. She hated needles. She waited until he was finished before speaking. He was pointing the gun at her head. "God is testing you, Charlie. Be sure you make the right decision."

She noticed his hesitation. She smiled at him, as calmly as she could.

"Why did the newspaper say you were in that group?" he asked.

She wasn't sure if he had researched it or not, so she chose her words carefully. "I joined while in law school, Charlie. How can we know our enemies if we don't infiltrate? I was also a secret member of The Women's Fellowship." She waited for that information to sink in and hoped that either there was such an organization or that he would believe there was.

He cocked his head to one side. *He's considering that. What else can I say?* She knew that he felt betrayed. Cathy had said as much. "I know you've been betrayed, Charlie. The mayor was a traitor to us. You did the right thing."

He lowered the gun just a bit. "Yes, he betrayed me. He was a Judas."

closed.

Toni opened her eyes, then closed them quickly. The bright lights hurt her head. "I take it I'm still alive," she said.

Claire laughed. "Yes, you are. But you've got a nasty wound there."

"Where's Boggs?"

"She's right here."

Toni was lying on her side on the gurney. She opened one eye and held out her hand. "Boggs?"

She felt the warmth of Boggs's hand in hers.

"I'm right here, babe."

Claire was behind Toni, working on the injury. "I just finished here, Toni. You needed a few stitches, but you should be fine."

"Did you mess up my hair?" Toni asked, smiling.

"Just a tad," Claire said. "Sorry about that. Nothing a little creative styling won't cure. Or a hat."

"Thanks, Claire."

Claire finished bandaging the area. "I'll leave you two alone for a bit," she said. "I want to find Vicky."

"It was Charlie," Toni whispered.

"I know, babe. He's dead."

"I remembered too late," Toni said.

"Remembered what?"

"Charlie played with his wedding ring. I saw it the first time I went, but I forgot." She closed her eyes. "I'm sorry."

Boggs kissed her on the cheek. "Don't be sorry, babe. You did good. You moved enough to miss the shot. You did really good. You rest for a bit, okay?"

"Will you stay with me? I just want to rest for a few minutes, then we can go home."

Boggs let go of her hand and pulled a chair up next to the gurney. "I'm not going anywhere," she said as she took Toni's hand again.

"I heard you say that before," Toni murmured. "Back there." She squeezed Boggs's hand and let herself drift off to sleep.

# Chapter 20

Toni opened her eyes on Wednesday morning in her own bed. It took only a second to realize that her head hurt. She reached up and felt the bandage. Boggs was sitting in a chair, looking at her.

Boggs jumped up and ran to the side of the bed. "Are you okay?"

"My head hurts a bit," Toni said. She looked at Boggs. "You look like crap. Did you stay up all night?"

Boggs nodded. "I was worried."

"What time is it?"

Boggs glanced at her watch. "It's only seven."

"I could use a cup of coffee," Toni said as she sat up. "And maybe some aspirin."

Boggs ran to the master bathroom and came back with a glass of water and a bottle. She handed the water to Toni and got out two pills. "Here." She had a prescription bottle.

"I don't think I need those," Toni said. She swung her feet

around and sat on the edge of the bed. The room went out of focus for a moment and her head throbbed. "On second thought, maybe I do." She reached out for the pills and quickly swallowed them.

"I'll go make coffee and bring it up to you," Boggs said.

"No, I want to go down. I'll just throw on some sweats and slippers and come down with you," Toni insisted. She touched the bandage on her head. "How bad is it?"

"You look beautiful," Boggs whispered, still holding her hand. "I was so afraid I'd lost you."

"Me, too, hon. Me, too." Toni kissed Boggs's hand.

"Claire put in thirteen stitches," Boggs said. "And I told her to be careful about how much hair she had to shave." Boggs laughed. "That was after I realized you'd be okay."

"Thirteen, huh?" Toni smiled. "Lucky number. And I think a baseball hat will cover it for now, don't you think?"

"You want to wear a hat now?"

"No, but when people come over tomorrow. I don't want my folks to worry."

Boggs nodded. "Are you sure you want to come down for coffee?"

"Absolutely," Toni said. "I don't want to miss one second of the rest of my life." She stood and felt a little wobbly. "And I need to work on our lists." She grinned. "Looks like you're going to be stuck going to the grocery store today."

Boggs handed her a pair of sweatpants and got her slippers out of the closet. "Nope. I already gave the list to Patty, who volunteered, I might add. I'm not leaving you for one second." They went down the stairs, arm in arm.

Toni sat at the island, waiting for the coffee to brew. She kissed Mr. Rupert's head so many times, he started to duck. Boggs brought her a cup of coffee, without Kahlúa, and made some toast. She had just finished eating when the doorbell rang. They both looked at the monitor. It was Vicky.

Vicky hugged Toni and handed her a bouquet of flowers. "I'm glad you're okay," she whispered after kissing her cheek.

"These are gorgeous," Toni said, handing them to Boggs. "They'll make the perfect centerpiece."

"Are you still doing Thanksgiving?" Vicky asked.

"Absolutely," Toni said.

Boggs put the flowers in a vase. "I asked her the same thing. You want a cup of coffee?"

Vicky nodded. "With a splash of something please. I'm celebrating." The smile on her face was contagious.

"You asked her, didn't you?" Toni asked.

Vicky nodded. "After what happened to you yesterday, I got the courage."

"What did she say? No, wait. What did you say?" Toni grinned. "Tell me *everything!*"

"Well," Vicky said. "It was after she sewed you up." She looked at Toni's head. "Nice job, by the way. Anyway, she came out of your room and I pulled her into the doctor's break room. Then I just blurted out that I loved her, like a real idiot."

"That's not being an idiot," Toni said.

Vicky took a sip of her coffee. "Jeez. Did you put *any* coffee in here, Boggs?" She grinned. "It's good. Anyway, then I did what you said, Toni. I handed her this tiny envelope with a key in it. She opened it and just stared at me. I thought I was going to throw up."

Toni laughed. "I bet. Did you say anything?"

"I told her I was giving her the key to my heart…and my house." Vicky smiled broadly.

"Pretty corny," Boggs said.

"Shut up," Vicky replied. "She said yes."

"I'm so happy for you guys," Toni said, hugging Vicky. "So she knows about the house and everything?"

Vicky nodded. "I showed her all the pictures I'd taken. She says she knows how to drywall." She grinned again. "I had to come by and tell you, and of course check to see how you are."

"Just a bit of a headache," Toni said. "And I haven't looked in the mirror yet."

"We went to Charlie's house last night," Vicky said. "His

mother was there and had no clue. We found a zip drive with all his crazy ideas."

"How did he get the insulin?" Boggs asked.

"According to his mother, his dead wife was a diabetic. I guess it just kept coming from a supply company. There were over thirty vials in the refrigerator in the garage."

Boggs shook her head. "I thought for sure it was Peter. I guess that means I still have to work with him."

"I wouldn't be so sure," Vicky said. "Captain Billings told me that he, Anne Mulhoney and Judge Crayton are looking into everyone that the mayor recommended for jobs. Apparently there are a few that lied on their applications, or that the mayor fast tracked without a proper background check."

"Boy, I bet Sam is chomping at the bit on that. Did you tell him?"

"Yup, I called him right after I talked to Captain Billings. He giggled like a girl." She finished her cup of coffee. "Okay, I've got to get going. Claire went back to her place to pick up some clothing and stuff."

"You've got the day off?" Toni asked.

"Yeah, after everything that happened, Captain Billings told me he'd see me on Monday." She stood to leave. "Guess I'll see you guys tomorrow. Take care of her, Boggs."

Boggs came back in the kitchen after letting Vicky out. She refilled their mugs of coffee. "This wasn't exactly how I planned on spending our day off," Boggs said, smiling. "But I'm glad you're okay."

Toni motioned for Boggs to come closer, then kissed her passionately. "Me, too, hon." She winked at Boggs. "Want to help me take a shower? I think I may need special help." She pointed to the bandage on her head.

Boggs raised her eyebrow, then grinned. "Whatever you need, babe."

They went up the stairs the same way they came down, arm in arm.

After lunch, Toni was stretched out on the couch, sipping hot tea. Patty had been true to her word and had arrived earlier with all the groceries. She'd told them that she considered flashing her badge to get through the long lines faster, but decided against it. The first turkey was already roasting in the oven and Toni was just beginning to smell it. She jumped when the doorbell rang.

Boggs was in the kitchen. "It's the delivery people with our tables and chairs," she said. "Stay there."

Toni did as instructed and watched as a young man and young woman carried the boxes into the living room. After the second trip, Toni looked more closely at the woman. She was wearing a baseball hat.

"Aren't you a law student?" Toni asked.

The woman put down the box. "Yes, ma'am. Third year."

"I thought I recognized you. It's Laurel, right?" Toni remembered her being one who always asked excellent questions.

"Yes, ma'am."

"You're in the clinic at Metro. And please, call me Toni."

"Yes, ma'am. I'm in the clinic. Just started this semester." The young woman said as she left to get another box.

When she returned, Toni smiled. "Prior military?" she asked.

"Yes, ma'am. How did you know?"

"You won't stop calling me ma'am," Toni said.

The young woman blushed. "Sorry. Habit." She went out for another box.

She and the young man came back with the final load. The young man went to Boggs with the paperwork. The young woman started to leave.

"Wait, Laurel," Toni said. "This is just a hunch, but do you have somewhere to go for Thanksgiving dinner?"

The young woman looked at the floor. "They're serving turkey at the dorms," she said.

"We would love for you to come here for dinner," Toni said. "We're having lots of people over and there's tons of food."

"That's awful nice of you, ma'am. But I couldn't impose."

"It's no imposition, really. It's just going to be a bunch of folks and football. We plan to start eating at two, but you can come over at noon. Of course that will mean that we'll put you to work."

Boggs had finished the paperwork and obviously overheard. "And we don't plan on finishing eating until dark," she added with a smile. "It will be fun."

"Are you sure?" Laurel asked.

"Positive," Toni said. "We'll see you tomorrow."

"Can I bring anything?"

"Nope, not a thing. We have everything we need."

"Especially since we now have tables and chairs," Boggs said.

Laurel's face lit up. "Okay. I will. Thank you very much." She left with the young man.

"You will invite anyone," Boggs said after kissing Toni. "I love that about you."

"She is one of the kids at the clinic," Toni said. "I've only talked to her a few times, but she seems really smart." She noticed that Boggs had one hand behind her back. "What are you hiding?"

"Just something," Boggs teased. "How bad do you want to see?"

Toni grinned and winked. "I'm not in the best of shape, but pretty bad."

Boggs presented Toni with a box.

She opened it quickly. "My shoes! New red shoes. Hey, I told you to cancel."

"But I couldn't resist," Boggs said. "I figured a girl can never have too many red shoes."

Toni pulled Boggs down on the couch and kissed her. "No wonder I love you so much. Not for the shoes, but for just being you."

"I know. Me, too. Here, try them on."

Toni slipped on her new red shoes and grinned. "They're perfect. Just like you and me. Perfect."

# Chapter 21

Toni woke up before the sun rose on Thanksgiving morning. Boggs and both the boys were still sleeping. She closed her eyes and thanked God for everything that she had, especially the love of the woman lying next to her. She slipped out of bed, careful not to wake Boggs, and pulled on her sweats. Mr. Rupert opened his eyes, and she motioned for him to follow. She put on her slippers and headed down to the kitchen with her furry companion on her heels.

She started a full pot of coffee, then got out a few bites of the turkey they'd fixed yesterday for Mr. Rupert. Her head was pounding, but she didn't care. She was alive and happy.

While the coffee brewed, she got out the twenty-two pound turkey and got it ready for the roaster. She wanted to make sure it was in the oven a little before eight. Once it was ready, she poured herself a cup of coffee and sat at the island with her list. Boggs appeared, looking like she'd only slept a couple hours.

"Hon, go back to sleep. I've got the turkey ready," Toni

insisted.

Boggs shook her head and wrapped her arms around Toni. "I don't want to miss one minute with you," Boggs said. "I can sleep anytime." She poured herself a cup of coffee and added Kahlúa and some half-and-half. "Do you want some in your coffee?"

"No, not right now," Toni said. "I took a couple pain pills. Maybe later."

Boggs stirred her coffee and looked at the end of the island near where Mr. Rupert was washing his face. "Hey! Is that turkey?"

Toni grinned. "I have no idea what you're talking about."

"If Mr. Rupert gets to sample turkey, then so do I," Boggs said as she opened the refrigerator. She turned to look at Toni. "Is it okay?"

"As long as you don't tell my mother," Toni whispered. "Give me a piece."

They drank their coffee and nibbled on turkey while going over their lists, trying to figure out what time the different casseroles should go in the oven.

"Let's go ahead and take showers now," Boggs said. "People might show up earlier than we think." She winked. "And I'm offering my services to help you. Since you're not supposed to get your head wet."

"That is *so* generous of you," Toni said. "Really going above and beyond the call of duty."

Boggs gave her a sharp salute. "At your service, ma'am."

Toni rolled her eyes. "But I'll take you up on that."

As they started up the stairs, Boggs said, "Speaking of ma'am, why did you ask that law student to dinner? Not that I mind at all. I was just curious."

"Aside from the fact that I thought she might be alone," Toni said, "Cathy told me that she saw me mentoring a young law student. And that this woman would go into politics. I think Laurel might be that woman."

"Interesting," Boggs said. "Come on, I'll mentor you in the shower."

Toni and Boggs were preparing their casseroles at about eleven o'clock when the doorbell rang. Toni glanced at the monitor. "Wow. That's early for Vicky and Claire." Boggs wiped off her hands and went to the door.

Vicky was carrying a large apple pie and Claire was lugging a large tote bag. They put their things on the island. "I hope you don't mind us coming early," Vicky said.

Toni hugged both of them. "Not at all. Happy Thanksgiving, and congratulations!"

Vicky was grinning from ear to ear, as was Claire.

"I've never been happier," Claire said. She kissed Vicky on the cheek. "Now let me look at your head."

After Claire announced that it was doing well, Toni got them each a cup of coffee. "You guys can either sit in here and watch us finish the casseroles, or you can make yourself comfy in the living room."

Vicky sat at the island. "Here is good." She sipped at her heavily spiked coffee. "We searched Charlie's office yesterday after I left here," she began. "He had a case of the Bibles there. They used them at the shelter."

"It's still hard to believe that it was Charlie," Toni said. "After all the times I talked to him."

"You said he gave you the creeps, though," Boggs said.

"Yeah, but I thought it was because he was such a bigot, not that he was our maniac," Toni said.

"None of us knew, Toni. Don't beat yourself up," Vicky said. "And I talked to Johnnie this morning. She found Irene Levitch."

Toni had finished the casserole and sat next to Claire at the kitchen island. "No kidding? Where?"

"She changed her life and her name," Vicky said. "She lives in St. Louis now and is working part-time and going to school. Johnnie said that after her assault, she knew she had to do something with her life."

"But why change her name?" Boggs asked.

"That was my question," Vicky said. "Apparently her parents were not the nicest or the most compassionate to her growing up, so she thought a name change would mark a new beginning for her."

"And it probably saved her life," Toni added. "I'm sure Charlie would have found her if she hadn't done that."

"Crazy son of a bitch," Vicky hissed.

"Okay, let's try to put all of this behind us and just be thankful we're all here together," Toni said.

They all agreed and after deciding there wasn't anything else they could do in preparation for dinner, they discussed Vicky and Claire's new home and what projects needed to be done.

The doorbell rang at ten minutes to twelve. "It's your folks," Boggs said.

Toni touched her head. "Crap. I'll run upstairs and get a hat. Boggs, you answer the door."

"Vicky, you better come with me," Boggs said. "It will take us several trips to bring everything in."

Toni ran out of the kitchen. She came back down wearing a Kansas City Chiefs baseball cap, just in time to help carry the second load of food from her parents' car. From that moment on, Toni was either fixing something in the kitchen or answering the door.

By one thirty that afternoon, all the guests had arrived and the tables had been put up in the living room. Football was playing on the television and there was a hum of happy conversations peppered with occasional laughter. Toni stopped what she was doing and took a moment to take in the whole scene. Her mom was in the kitchen next to Boggs, each one preparing something. Her dad was sitting in the living room, teasing Vicky about her football team. All of her friends were gathered together, and the smell of wonderful food mixed with the burning logs on the fire. She caught Boggs's eye and motioned for her to come into the mudroom.

"Are you okay, babe? Are you in pain?" Boggs looked a little worried.

"No, hon. I'm fine." She kissed her. "I just wanted to have thirty seconds alone with you before we eat. I wanted to tell you how much I love you and how thankful I am to have you in my life. And to thank you."

"Thank me for what?"

"For loving me," Toni whispered. She touched Boggs's cheek and kissed her.

Boggs hugged her. "This is our first annual Thanksgiving dinner," she whispered back. "I hope we have fifty more."

They went back to the kitchen, arm in arm.

SIDE ORDER OF LOVE by Tracey Richardson. Television foodie star Grace Wellwood is not going to be golf phenom Torrie Cannon's side order of romance for the summer tour. No, she's not. Absolutely not. $13.95

WORTH EVERY STEP by KG MacGregor. Climbing Africa's highest peak isn't nearly so hard as coming back down to earth. Join two women who risk their futures and hearts on the journey of their lives. $13.95

WHACKED by Josie Gordon. Death by family values. Lonnie Squires knows that if they'd warned her about this possibility in seminary, she'd remember. $13.95

BECKA'S SONG by Frankie J. Jones. Mysterious, beautiful women with secrets are to be avoided. Leanne Dresher knows it with her head, but her heart has other plans. Becka James is simply unavoidable. 13.95

GETTING THERE by Lyn Denison. Kat knows her life needs fixing. She just doesn't want to go to the one place where she can do that: home. $13.95

PARTNERS by Gerri Hill. Detective Casey O'Connor has had difficult cases, but what she needs most from fellow detective Tori Hunter is help understanding her new partner, Leslie Tucker. 13.95

AS FAR AS FAR ENOUGH by Claire Rooney. Two very different women from two very different worlds meet by accident--literally. Collier and Meri find their love threatened on all sides. There's only one way to survive: together. $13.95